Paolo Antonio Magrì

RESCUE CODE

ISBN: 978-1-911424-89-5
SKU/ID: 9781911424895

All Rights Reserved. No part of this book can be used or reproduced in any manner whatsoever without written permission from the publisher, except in the case of brief quotations embodied in critical articles or reviews.
A catalogue record for this book is available from the British Library.

Editor: Wolf Graham
Layout: Wolf Graham
Cover: Wolf Graham
Translation: Charlotte J. March
Font: Plantin MT Std
Edwardian Script ITC
28 Days Later
Arial

Publishing Company:
Black Wolf Edition & Publishing Ltd.
Scotland (UK)
www.blackwolfedition.com

Copyright © 2020 by Black Wolf Edition & Publishing Ltd.
and other respective owners identified in this work.
Designs and Patents Act 1988
All rights reserved.
First Edition 2020 - First Printing 2020

"With deep feeling to my wife Giusy, for her constant support and precious suggestions."

Prologue

'I said I want it!'

'The third attempt failed like the others, sir. We've exhausted our resources.'

'That's not my problem. I want it. Do I need to remind you how many billions of dollars are at stake? Moreover, we have not exhausted the possibilities of completing the project. There would be the last one.'

'You mean...'

'I mean that one.'

'Sir, do you have any idea what you're asking me?'

'I have an idea! I remind you that I'm not paying you to argue, but to execute.'

'Do you understand that the real problem is the second phase of the project?'

'I'm counting on your willingness and discretion. As you know, you cannot deny me your services.'

'Certainly, sir. I have only one question to ask.'

'Go ahead, you deserve it.'

'Which of the two systems do you intend to use?'

'Well, that's for you to decide. You're the magician.'

'I'd play it safe and use the physiological. I wouldn't risk it with the accelerator. It will take a few years, but the result is guaranteed.'

'Gone! Good luck with your work.'

'May God forgive us, sir.'

'He's already forgiven us, don't worry. That's all.'

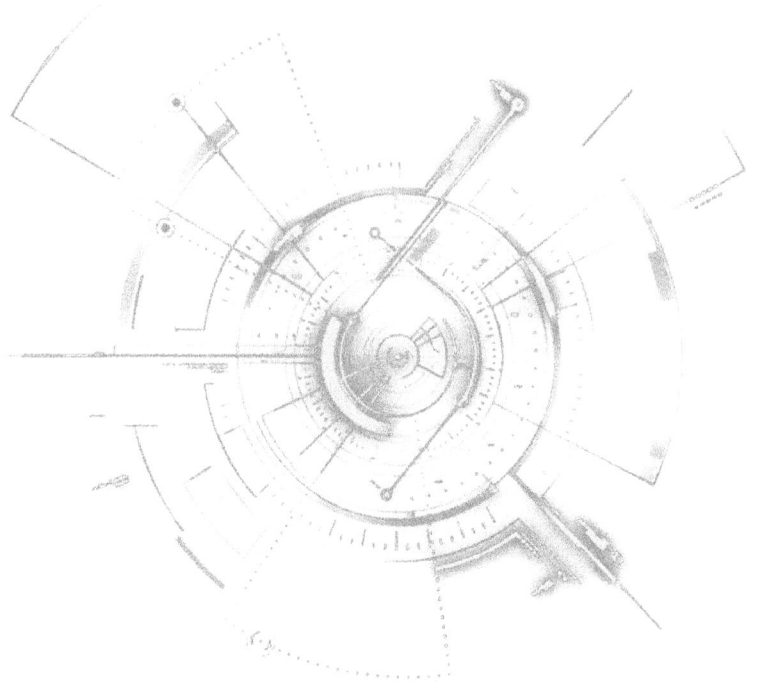

CHAPTER 1

Twenty-nine years later

The sun dominated the horizon and the temperature, stable at fourteen degrees, was ideal for morning jogging. A wonderful army of fir trees seemed to be escorting the path that ran along the forest. No human presence within 100 kilometres. The water in the lake was flat, only sometimes shaken by an almost imperceptible breeze. Acting as a soundtrack, the chirping of birds.

It was Daniel's favourite environment whenever he found the time, or rather the desire, to set the laziest legs of the university in motion. He didn't like running very much, but it was the only way to keep fit and keep his weight down.

Once the warm-up was over, he had started to grind kilometres and now, after thirty minutes of fast running, the attention for the wrist monitor was gone.

The surrounding environment was certainly more interesting, from the small deer playing with each other along the lake shore to the flight of the birds, from the chromatic nuances of the flowers to the melodies of nature in the background. To the north, a faint waterfall seemed to caress a rock face, almost as if to sweeten its harshness.

For Daniel, every time was like the first time. He was punctually enraptured by the panorama that accompanied him and even that morning, almost without realizing it, he reached the usual bifurcation: on the right, he would find a path inside a wheat field, on the left a road that crossed a fishing village.

The path chosen most frequently was the one on the left,

as it offered the greatest range of colours. The blue of the river, the yellow of the shacks, the green of the woods, surrounded by the gurgling of the streams, constituted an extraordinary panel of sensory stimuli. On the shore an old man, with a grey beard and hollowed-out eyes, was playing with some children. In the distance Daniel could see the fishermen's wives.

He was still uncertain which path to take when the whole landscape suddenly became dark. Total darkness. The river is gone, the shacks with the woods are gone, the children are gone. Everything and everyone around swallowed up by darkness.

'Damn it!' he exclaimed then, disappointed he couldn't do the whole jogging session.

Once again, the Running Globe had stalled. The emergency lights had switched on and the red ERROR sign on the front of the big screen reigned.

After a few seconds, Miss Carson, the housekeeper, was ready to suffer the professor's rash. The script was always the same.

'Cursed be the day I bought this Globe, Miss Carson,' he began. 'You are not to blame, you bought the best, it can happen,' replied the housekeeper as protocol. 'That can't happen when you spend $100,000 and buy a Mikiton,' continued Daniel. 'You're right, Professor,' closed Miss Carson, diluting the excitement of what she might consider, with good reason, more than an employer, and announcing that breakfast was ready.

Actually, Daniel had a point. He had bought the best Running Globe on the market, the only one that could simultaneously set the height of the sun on the horizon, air temperature, wind speed and direction, type of fauna and flora, alternative paths, type of waterfalls, chirping, plus a thousand other devilry simulated by a fibre optic sphere – the Globe – which virtualized from all perspectives.

Mikiton's Running Globe was the best solution for those who didn't like or couldn't run outdoors. Therefore, it was understandable a reaction like that. Daniel was also superstitious and did not forget that his day had turned out to be very bad, on the two occasions when the Globe had jammed.

'Please call for assistance,' the professor graciously ordered.

'It will be done,' replied Miss Carson, reaffirming the breakfast was ready.

The word "breakfast" always put him in a good mood, and was the housekeeper's ace up her sleeve when she wanted to bring him back to calm.

Daniel considered himself a health nut, so his breakfast was the same as his great-great-grandmother's: bread, butter, jam and milk. All strictly non transgenic.

Antoinette Carson's breakfast was among the best in the world and could sweeten even a sharp man like Professor Keaton. In the opinion of the elderly housekeeper, this angularity was only a rough rind that protected a noble and sweet soul. According to her, who could have been a psychologist as a second job, everything was connected to his relationship with his father and she had more than half an idea about the causes.

At nine o'clock on the dot, as usual, the professor said goodbye also that morning and left the house to go to the university. He took his envied car and headed for work.

The Criton 200SF was an M-Car for true connoisseurs and especially for *retro* style fanatics. The design was that of the cars of a hundred years before, also for the interior equipment, but it concealed a first-class technological apparatus.

It had cost him quite a bit of money, after all, he could afford it and it wasn't the only thing he could give himself in life. His excellent financial position came from the inheritance he received, as an only child, from his parents: his father, a lawyer, and his mother, a doctor, had paved the way for him, allowing him, among other things, to graduate from the best university in the state.

Except for the period of his studies, he had always lived in his family's villa, in one of the medium-density residential blocks, far from the chaos of N-Town and the squalor of O-Town.

After the death of his parents, he had kept Miss Carson, a true pillar of the house, in service, and had decided to take up the pleasant role of the golden bachelor.

The Criton's on-board computer, meanwhile, reported that he was right on schedule, that he was crossing O-Town and would enter N-Town after four minutes twenty-five seconds.

'I can see for myself that I'm going through O-Town,' thought Daniel. 'I'm not blind.'

The display indicated parameters and coordinates:

TRANSIT LEVEL: FOUR
ARRIVAL TIME: 09.22 AM
DESTINATION: UNIVERSITY OF HIRE CITY

He knew that too.

The precise details of the on board computer were useless to him, but he loved to be told all the same, for the pleasure of one day witnessing some of its mistakes. Quite unlikely, he realized.

The university was in area five of the first block of N-Town.

O-Town and N-Town stood for Old Town and New Town. They were the main agglomerations of Hire City, the state capital. Many also called them Black Town and White Town, because they were white against black: two realities light years apart, two worlds at the antipodes.

Old Town was the history and the old of Hire City, in fact, in its streets people continued to live essentially as a hundred years before. It developed mainly with steel skyscrapers arranged in a chequered pattern and divided by narrow streets, which allowed only old hydrogen-powered cars to circulate. The brand new and super technological M-Car, the magnetic levitation cars, required much larger spaces and above all a different urban architecture.

N-Town was the new part of Hire City. An army of one hundred and thirty gigantic transparent parallelepipeds, the Big Blocks, spread evenly along the banks of the Himming River, which divided the city in two, then sewn up by the dense array of tube-gates, huge cylindrical passages that connected the blocks on the east side with those on the west side.

The most famous of these was the Big Gate, immediately renamed Hacker Gate because hackers were able to hologram their more or less artistic, and more or less legal, works inside it.

Canning humankind had been inevitable to make amends for past mistakes. If it had taken time to create the damage, much more would have been needed to remedy a crazy environmental policy that had made the climate hostile to man and his activities.

The so-called "global reconversion process" lasted thirty years, during which the less fortunate had to succumb to the unfortunate weather conditions, waiting for the main metropolises to be caged. To pay the highest price in human lives, as it was obvious that it would happen in such circumstances, were the poorest countries, forced to beg for the hospitality of the great rich nations, the only ones able to finance and carry out a project of such dimensions and who fixed the sites of the new gigalopolis, of course, in their own territories.

On the 29th April 2092, the Council of Crisis decreed the end of the protection process. The NEW DAY, or more concisely N-Day, marked the beginning of a new era for humanity.

Once the first phase had been completed, that is that of canning and the removal of humankind from climatic aggression, in the following decades we saw the abnormal expansion of the only thirty-one States still existing on planet Earth.

The buildings enclosed by the first Blocks maintained their original physiognomy and over time they became browned in a slow, continuous and inexorable decay. In every gigalopolis they ended up becoming the "old city", a refuge for desperate and gangsters.

The new Blocks, on the other hand, experienced unprecedented economic, technological, demographic and urban development.

CHAPTER 2

At 9:28 a.m. Daniel Keaton was already in front of the entrance to the W255 classroom.

The lesson of that 2nd February 2256 would have been remembered all his life. The study programme for the day included discussion of the popular uprisings and political unrest in Europe in the 22nd century against human cloning projects.

The lesson was, as usual, dominated by authority and enthusiasm at the same time, marked by lively discussions between students who supported conflicting opinions, and accompanied by the winks of the students bewitched by his charm.

Professor Keaton's lectures were famous for the active role reserved for the gyys, whose judgments were stimulated and listened to and then centrifuged into the debate that characterized the last twenty minutes. Even that day two hours had flown by. The issue of cloning projects and the moral question it raised were still topical, even though all those years had passed.

Punctual, as it had begun, at eleven thirty the lesson ended. As he left the classroom, Daniel was approached by a young woman. She didn't give the impression of being a student, she showed no more than thirty or thirty-five years. The golden blonde hair grazed the shoulders with a soft bob. The slim body, with an elegant posture, was embellished by two ultramarine blue eyes and a charm that was independent of the external appearance. The clothing was strictly designer: grey trousers, red blouse, high heel but not dizzy shoes.

'Professor Keaton, I need to talk to you,' the young lady

said without even saying hello. She seemed to be in a hurry and kept looking nervously around. 'Excuse me! Good morning, my name is Katrine Johnson and I need at all costs to speak with you' she corrected herself.

'Good morning,' he replied a little uncertain, yet smiling.

'Can we go to your studio, please? It's something delicate.'

'All right.'

Daniel's studio was on the same floor, squeezed at the end of a blind corridor that ended straight at his shelter. He had demanded from the rector just that, since it allowed him to escape from the confusion and buzz of the people. His lair was not excessively large, but well organized and above all full of books, school texts, publications and manuals. 'A true rarity for true connoisseurs', the person concerned often said; 'for true fanatics', others specified; 'for archeopsychopaths', the most polemical advocates claimed.

At a time when thousands of books could be immediately available on a memory of a few millimetres, he still insisted on using old paper books. Those crammed in his studio were only part of the library he could show off at home. When some of his most trusted friends found the courage to point out this strange passion of his, he would take refuge in the corner kick with the old and proven excuse of investing in publishing antiques.

Daniel and Katrine Johnson walked down the endless corridor. The professor typed in the password, the security system swallowed the password and the door opened. Once inside, he made the girl sit down and consumed the ritual of every morning: opening the curtains, deactivating the drawer block, and anxiously searching for the irreplaceable orange candy, which he immediately offered his guest.

'Would you like that, miss?'

'Ma'am. No, thank you.'

'Tell me how I can help you,' continued Daniel.

'I'd like to find out what you have to do with my life.'

A sentence like that, with neither head nor tail, could only imply two eventualities: he was dealing with a psychopath, or that was a joke. In both cases, it was better not to overreact, in order to avoid bad reactions. He remained calm and relaxed, especially in tone. He flaunted a circumstantial smile, stroked his beard and asked, 'Could you be more specific, please?'

'It's a complicated story. If I had figured it out, I wouldn't have come all the way over here.'

The young girl's face began to darken. She added, 'The only thing I'm sure of...is that you are somehow connected to my family, and perhaps to my husband's disappearance. Actually, the only thing I know is that you... I mean... I mean... It's like if...You...'

'All right, that's enough,' interrupted Daniel, managing to block out that rash of rambling phrases. It seemed that the woman feared that she could not finish a speech before she had even started it, so the words flew from her lips and remained meaningless.

'I have little time to explain. Believe me, I'm not crazy,' she continued, gesturing in growing agitation. Daniel was impressed, and somehow scared. Katrine Johnson did not seem dangerous, but she was clearly altered, perhaps prey to some strange substance. Or maybe she was a mythomaniac. It certainly wasn't for him to find out.

'Miss, I'm here to receive the students and the colleagues, not to...'

'Does the name Robert Konnor mean anything to you? He was my husband. You have something to do with football? I'm a doctor and I found out that...'

Daniel stiffened and waved a hand to silence her.

'Listen, I work here. If you have any questions about my profession, ask, otherwise go away. I've already pressed the button to call security, though.'

Katrine Johnson realized she had exhausted her chance to be heard.

'All right,' hissed bitterly. 'I hope to come back if they'll give me the chance.'

She got up, opened the door and left. The communicator rang at the same time.

'I accept,' said Daniel to activate the holographic call.

That was Mr Finson, head of security.

'Professor Keaton, a problem has been brought to our attention. You may be bothered by a person. Keep the door locked. I'll send an officer to you right away.'

'All right.'

'Out.'

The lapidary conclusion of the call upset him. Mr Finson used to call him 'Professor Daniel,' after all, they'd known each other for years. Secondly, who and why did you report the girl's presence? He only pretended to call security in the presence of Mrs Johnson.

A knock on the door took him away from those thoughts. Finson's warning advised him to keep closed, but after a few moments of reflection, his instinct took over and he decided to open up.

Behind the door, Katrine Johnson awaited him again. She was lying on the ground, powerless. She probably tried to get to the door with the last of her energy and ended up banging into it. Her face looked contracted, her eyes grainy and shiny. Daniel called her, no answer. He looked around lost, but there was no one around. He noticed the woman was holding a circuit board. Weird. Different from the common ones. He opened her palm and took it.

The hand stayed open, taut. Daniel bent over the woman and tried to wrap her in his own, as if to support her. After making the effort to lift her arm, Katrine grazed the professor's astonished face trembling. Then she lowered her eyelids and her facial expression became more relaxed. It wasn't clear whether she was unconscious or dead. There were, in any case, no traces of blood, apparent signs of a struggle or wounds.

Daniel tried to call for help with his communicator, but it seemed out of order. He decided, then, to go in person and ask for help. The nearest point of support was the security office.

He hurried down the corridor that separated him from the rest of the world and, upon arriving in the main hall, rushed to Mr Finson's office.

In the excitement, he risked overwhelming a man coming from the opposite direction, apologized and continued at a steady pace. Daniel broke into the security office.

'Mr Finson, I need your help. That woman is unconscious in front of my office. We need to alert the EMT. My Olo-Com doesn't work, you call it.'

'I don't know which woman you're talking about, but I'll get right on it,' Finson replied, immediately activating the communicator. 'This is Finson, security. There is an unconscious woman in front of Professor Daniel Keaton's office. I request immediate intervention. Top priority.'

Having fulfilled his duty, Finson advised Daniel to go back with him to the studio and wait for help there.

Along the way, the professor resumed the speech of the warning call he had received a few minutes earlier.

'Mr Finson, this is probably about the woman who flagged me. I didn't heed your warning because she had just left and then...'

'What are you talking about, Professor Daniel?'

'Well, it was you who told me not to...'

That sentence died in their nips: they had just arrived near the studio, but there was no girl in front of the door.

Finson looked at him.

'She's gone! But believe me, she was there.'

'Describe the girl, Professor Daniel,' the head of security shot.

His tone didn't sound incredulous, so he wasn't in danger of passing for crazy. Daniel tried to be as precise as possible.

'She was a woman in her 30s, blonde, straight hair down to her shoulders, blue eyes, fair complexion. She was alive, but weak, and very stiff. If I hadn't had the chance to meet her just a few minutes earlier, I'd swear she was paralyzed.'

'I bet she could barely move her eyes,' Finson speculated.

'It's true. I was just about to tell you. How do you know that?'

'It's the classic effect of the B3KR, one of the most powerful electro drugs being shot nowadays. She must have exaggerated with the calibration. The effect can last from a few seconds to several minutes. The girl probably ran away so she wouldn't get caught. She's risking ten years in jail. Anyway, we'll know more as soon as I see the CCTV recording.'

Finson took his communicator and called Ops.

'Currie, it's Finson. Prepare the recording for the corridor 325, I'll be there as soon as...'

The cop's voice stopped and his face went dark. He listened.

'Did something happen?' Daniel intervened after Finson shut down the communication.

'The systems in the entire sector have been disabled by a magnetic shock. Someone sabotaged the system, so we can't get the recording. That's why his communicator wasn't working. I will try to extract something from the shooting of the adjacent sectors and the last profit of the 325. In the meantime, I'd advise you to go home and keep your eyes open. I salute you.'

Daniel had stayed to listen to the agent's telegraphic report and was only able to return the greeting as he left. He wanted to ask a few questions, but he couldn't ask any. He felt strangely shaken up, too many things didn't add up that morning.

However, the advice to go home seemed like a really good idea. There were no other classes scheduled for that day, and as for the paperwork...they could wait an extra day. He closed the studio, crossed the long corridor and headed towards the sixty-seven elevator. Waiting patiently in the cabin, he zigzagged the three thousand five hundred meters that separated the university building from the parking area. He got out of that crystal box and found himself just a few steps away from his M-Car: he had been given the best parking space in the whole car park.

Once in the cockpit, he didn't feel like driving. Activated the autopilot, selected HOME, pulled the head to the headrest and tried to recover some mental energy.

The on board computer confirmed the success of the operation.

   AUTOMATIC MODE ACTIVATED
     HOME ROUTE ONLINE
  START NAVIGATION IN FOUR SECONDS

The display stunted the short countdown.
Four.
Three.
Two.
One.
The vehicle moved.
Daniel closed his eyes.

Chapter 3

'Mission accomplished. Anomaly removed. Over and out.'
The tension in his voice loosened.
'Trenton, patch me through to the base and get me a hot chocolate.'
The young man immediately stood to attention.
'At your command, Captain. I'll get right on it.'
The chocolate came from an efficient vending machine that was just a few meters from his desk, but having Trenton bring it to him had a particular taste. After a whole week spent taking orders from people who were several degrees below him, a healthy and small regurgitation of authority was healthy for the captain.
Trenton knew it and went along with it. After all, he deserved respect and gratitude. The captain had helped him on several occasions. Beyond appearances, his superior was not authoritarian and always established a relationship of collaboration on an equal footing with the men of the teams that, from time to time, were entrusted to him. His way of setting up the work was a guarantee of synergy and effectiveness.
'Here's your chocolate, sir. The link to the base will be active in thirty seconds. It took longer than usual, we had to dodge an intercept attempt.'
'Okay Trenton, you can go,' awarded the graduate, pleased with the infallible accuracy of his best collaborator. The captain sat down, placed the hot cup on the table and programmed the receiver to "wait". A few seconds went by and Lieutenant Summer's image appeared on the screen in front. His voice resounded loud and clear.

'This is base, Lieutenant Summer at your complete disposal, Captain.'

'Good morning Lieutenant, I just wanted to know if the subject has been withdrawn from the cover area.'

'Certainly, Captain. He's already with the others.'

'Condition?'

'Stationary, Captain. Our team is confident, but it will take time. A little more and we would have lost him.'

'I know. But the unit that came in first wasn't part of the team and I couldn't control it. I'm counting on you for recovery time. It's important for the operation.'

'Certainly, Captain. We'll do our best.'

'All right, I salute you, Lieutenant Summer.'

'Good day, Cap...'

Communication suddenly broke down. Darkness.

The captain remained impassive. He already knew what it could be, and he made sure of it as soon as everything was reactivated. The diligent Trenton was already at the door.

'Still the same problem, Trenton?'

'Yes, Captain. They went over it with a new magnetic scanning system, so I had to disable all our devices to avoid their detection. Now they can reach beyond our depths.'

'Well done, Trenton.'

The young lieutenant nodded, pleased not so much with the compliment he received as with the personal satisfaction of evading his opponent for the umpteenth time. The success of the entire operation was also linked to their ability to hide.

'I have an important communication to make to you,' continued the captain. 'You'll be in charge of the team while I'm gone. Tomorrow should start the second part of the plan.'

'Aye aye, Captain. I'll do my best.'

'That's it, you can go.'

Trenton walked away smiling.

Chapter 4

The penetrating hiss of the alarm clock forced Daniel to get up. It was 17:00.

It was the first time in many years that he gave in to an afternoon siesta. His afternoons were usually devoted to reading the classics of the 21st century.

That day he had decided to abandon himself to Morpheus not so much for tiredness, but to force himself not to think. The hours would have gone by faster that way.

A question from Mrs Johnson kept hammering his brain: *'Do you have anything to do with football?'*

The word "football" flipped a little switch. Those six letters awakened painful memories and conflicting feelings, still alive even though thirty years had passed.

He tried to drive them away. 'I don't have to think about it, it was better that way,' he repeated again, pretending as usual to believe it. He got up and headed for the bathroom, hoping that a cold shower would stop that bleeding of images.

She stayed under the water for a long time, offering his face. Gradually the thoughts loosened their grip and seemed to retreat in good order.

He dried quickly, put on the clothes he had put on a stool, and went back to his room. When he put aside his dirty clothes, something fell on the floor: the electronic card he had collected from the paralyzed hands of that strange girl. That type of card has not been used as an access key, or for other uses, for at least a hundred years. What to do with it, then?

The card was white and on the top it had a logo formed

by the intersection of two letters: the U and the B. If it had been a modern card, he would have instinctively deduced that those letters indicated the Union Bank, one of the largest credit institutions in Hire City. That, however, was a card worthy of the science museum and the Union Bank was only fifty years old. Impossible, then.

Yet Katrine Johnson had wanted to give it to him with her last strength, it had to have an intrinsic importance.

The temptation to figure out where that card would lead him was enormous. The upside was that, even if he wanted to, he couldn't do anything. Except for her first and last name, maybe fake, he knew nothing about that woman, much less her address.

The alibi that was packaged to quell curiosity seemed to hold up.

Miss Carson's timely intervention interrupted those thoughts.

'Professor Daniel, your tea is ready.'

'Yes, thank you. I'll be right there.'

He put the electronic card in his pocket and left his room.

The 17:10 appointment was one of the professor's favourite psychophysical pit stops. Strictly non-transgenic, tea and butter cookies have accompanied his afternoon break for more than twenty years.

The ten-minute shift with respect to the rite of Anglo-Saxon origin was due solely to the singular stubbornness to refuse, per party taken, any form of homologation.

Incidentally, the time was well matched with the live edition of the 17:15 news. He loved to follow it right in the dining room, on the holographic maxi-screen, the only technology not to be camouflaged in a two-thousand-years-style environment. The floor, and not only the dining room floor, was made of real parquet, as were the wall coverings and the curtains on the windows. Nonconformist to the extreme, continuing the tradition of the Keaton family had not succumbed to the flattery of surfaces that allowed, if necessary and with a simple remote control, to change the finishes with the same ease with which you could change the program on TV.

Daniel sat at the head of the long table in the middle of the room. The acrid but pleasant scent of lemon pervaded her nostrils. He activated the screen.

'OPEN! Channel One!'

Just in time for the news. He began to enjoy his tea.

'Good morning and welcome to News One. We open this afternoon edition, unfortunately, with sad news. Katrine Johnson, wife of the famous football player Robert Konnor, who disappeared into thin air just two months ago, took her own life. For details, let's connect with Carla Dikon, our correspondent from Hire City.'

Daniel startled me. For the second time in a few hours, Katrine Johnson's name came crashing down on him.

'This is Carla Dikon, from Hire City. Perhaps she couldn't stand the pain of her husband's disappearance: this is the most credible thesis by the police that this morning found the body of Katrine Johnson, lifeless, in her Regent Street home. Only two months ago the famous football player Robert Konnor, "The King" as he was nicknamed, mysteriously disappeared. The woman's husband, after monopolizing the sports news for more than ten years, had suddenly lost track of him last 29 November. So many theories put forward about his disappearance, but none have ever caught on to the investigators. Today the first, and certainly the most serious, consequence of that mystery: the suicide of his wife, Dr Katrine Johnson, head physician at Central Hospital in Hire City. An extreme gesture that no one could and could not guess. Speaking with colleagues at the hospital, we have recorded

some testimonies that present us with a very serene Katrine Johnson. There! I'm told by the director that we are also able to offer you the images provided by the police, regarding the discovery of the body. They can air them.'

The images depicted Johnson's body crouching on the floor of her house. The pale complexion and blond hair contrasts sharply with the colour of the floor.

A brief interview with a detective was then broadcast, reaffirming the confidentiality of the investigation.

'*We're pursuing all avenues, but we're favouring suicide. That's all I can say.*'

In closing, the interviews with colleagues at Central Hospital, who expressed astonishment at such an unexpected gesture.

'*Certainly the disappearance of her husband was a blow to her. But it seemed to me that she had already managed to find a certain balance,*' said a colleague from her team.

Among the faces running through the filming at Central Hospital, Daniel would have expected to recognize one familiar to him. He was disappointed.

Meanwhile, the images were finished and the line was back to the reporter.

'*It's all from Regent Street. If there is any news, we will give you an account of it in the next link. For News One, Carla Dikon, Hire City.*'

'*Thank you, Carla. We continue now with the other news. Minister of Culture Tommy...*'

Daniel's voice command immediately dissolved the images.

That news unhinged the cage that his common sense had created around him to force him not to think, and above all to erase the image of that woman. He could no longer regard the whole day as a series of fortuitous events. The person who showed up in front of him that morning wasn't just anybody, but a doctor at Central Hospital. Besides, she was telling the truth about her husband.

Therefore, it was impossible not to link the morning's events to the woman's suicide. Any rational person would know something wasn't right.

Nervousness was growing. Daniel wasn't used to being overwhelmed by events. He used to keep track of things and facts. He preferred to rationalize and manage them.

'Professor Daniel!'

The housekeeper was trying to get his attention. He shook his head, already fed up with all those riddles. The tone of his voice betrayed some tiredness.

'What is it, Miss Carson?'

'The police are asking for you. He's downstairs. He's a Detective Torst.'

'Send him up, miss.'

'As you wish.'

The invitation given by the professor proved superfluous: the policeman had already faced the imposing daily staircase overlooking the central entrance, and was right behind Miss Carson.

'Good morning, Professor Keaton. I apologize for the intrusion, but I'm in a hurry and duty requires me to run. Don't be upset if I didn't wait for your housekeeper's permission.'

Daniel answered with the usual courtesy.

'Good morning, Detective. No problem. Please, have a seat.'

The first sensation was to have already crossed that face, but it quickly disappeared.

'Miss Carson, you may go.'

'Certainly, Professor.'

The policeman had already occupied the sofa under the middle window of the room. Daniel preferred to sit in the chair in front.

'Tell me how I can help you, Detective,' he said with a relaxed attitude.

'I'll be brief: we understand that a woman named Katrine Johnson came to see you in your study this morning. The doctor was found dead a few hours ago.'

'Yes, I heard the news on the news.'

'Better that way, you'll spare me the details. You understand, then, that it is very important for us to receive any information about her visit. What did Katrine Johnson want from you?'

It was perhaps the most eagerly awaited question from Daniel's selfish half, who couldn't wait to shake off the burden of having to figure something out for himself. Telling his strange morning, he would delegate everything to the police and continue his ordinary life.

The battling half, doubtful, suspicious, curious and repressed for years, instead asked for clarity and above all pretended to get to the truth without outside help.

The selfish half won the game.

'Detective Torst, I might say today was a very strange morning.'

'What do you mean, "strange"?'

Torst adjusted himself to the armchair, leaning forward and showing a keen interest in that preamble.

Daniel stared better at his guest and suddenly remembered where he had already seen him. He was the person he'd clashed with at the university on his way to the security office.

What was Detective Torst doing there, by the way, seconds before Katrine Johnson disappeared from the landing of her office, right at the mouth of the access corridor?

The cop already knew about their meeting, which is why he showed up at his house so soon after Johnson's body was found.

Detective Torst was at best pretending not to know for investigative purposes.

'It's the way the police operate,' thought Daniel, but the curious reaction of the policeman had left him, from the very beginning, with some doubts. He had no concrete evidence to support his distrust, but his sixth sense seemed to alarm him.

The battalion half, suffocated a few seconds earlier, finally had what it takes to take over the other. He decided to lie.

'You see, Detective... In all my years of teaching, I've never had a doctor as accomplished as Dr Johnson come to me and ask me to tutor her in history class.'

Torst's expression showed disbelief mixed with disappointment. To appear more credible, Daniel added more details to his story.

'By the way, Detective, I believe the request for tutoring was an excuse and aimed at something else. I haven't had a chance to check, either, but I bet that woman wasn't enrolled in college at all.'

'I understand, Professor Keaton,' replied the policeman, in the tone of someone who'd drilled a hole in the water. 'But she didn't tell you anything else? Something beyond the first request and somehow revealing her true purpose?'

Daniel pretended to think about it for a few moments, then he shook his head and Torst had to capitulate.

'All right, Professor. I hope I haven't taken up too much of your time. This is my business card, if you remember anything else please do not hesitate to contact me, even for details that may seem irrelevant to you.'

'Count on it, Detective. You will be the first to be informed,' lied Daniel, who couldn't wait to get rid of him. The policeman, meanwhile, had got up and headed for the door.

The landlord walked him to the main hall, leaving him in Miss Carson's care. She was going to lead him out.

Having fulfilled his duties, Daniel rushed to the studio. He activated the CCTV monitors and made sure that the policeman left the villa, escorting him with his eyes to the outside. Then he abandoned himself in his chair.

The decision was made: he had to get to the bottom of it. He probably would have found the answers at Katrine Johnson's house. He was going to try the next day. It was his day off, so his absence would avoid arousing suspicion in Faculty.

Chapter 5

'We recovered three more.'

'Bravo.'

'If you hadn't come along and told us how to do it, we'd only have saved only one, by accident.'

A sense of satisfaction veiled his response.

'The more numerous we are, the more likely we are to get out of this cesspool.'

He read on the face of the interlocutor an understandable and respectful hesitation, so he hastened to clarify.

'You just need a little more patience. We're going to get out of here. I promised you. You don't want to give in now that we're close to our goal?'

His determination had the desired effect.

'I obey, champ.'

In response to the joking tone, he pretended to throw the maps on the table. Then the atmosphere became serious again.

'Now we work.'

'All right.'

Chapter 6

The Chief's office was located on the 327th floor. Like all respected commanders, he too had decided to place himself above his own army.

According to the most informed rumours, the charm of the White Room, as it was nicknamed the most famous office of the Block, was due to the concentration of the best technologies and above all to the halo of mystery that surrounded it, since only a select few had had the honour, or misfortune according to others, to enter it.

The position offered by the top floor was among the most suggestive and the visual control over Hire City was total. The access to the Block's most disturbing and feared office was provided by a unique and confidential antigravity elevator. There were only two options on the floor selection wall: EARTH on the left side, a blue dot on the right side. Torst touched the part marked with the blue dot. The walls of the elevator changed appearance and became the same colour. After two seconds, he started moving.

The initial sensation was of being crushed downwards, but it only took a few moments for the body to adjust to the acceleration.

Arriving at the 376th floor, the elevator stopped and the doors opened. Torst went out and headed in the only possible direction, taking a long tunnel that opened right at the exit of the elevator.

The atmosphere offered was almost burial. On the walls it was proposed the holographic projection of some individuals, probably important personalities but unknown to him. The straight was then interrupted by tortuous passages and an alternating sequence of steps and landings. Once the last sensor beam has passed unscathed, the laser shielding protecting the end section of the corridor dissolved. Further on, an oversized security man stood between him and what was most likely the entrance to the White Room.

'That's Detective Torst, I suppose,' recited the big man nailed to the door.

'Yes, it's me.'

'The boss is waiting for you.'

'I got here as fast as I could.'

The agglomeration of muscles approached the detective and put his hand inside his uniform. The gesture worried Torst, but he remained impassive.

The man pulled out an eye scanner. He put it to his face. Shortly afterwards the red LED on the handle turned green and echoed an anonymous beep.

'You may go in now.'

The guard moved and left room for a door without a handle, which opened by itself. Torst took a few steps and entered.

The image that appeared before him was that of a huge box with white walls, completely bare and without the apparent presence of corners. He immediately understood why it was called the White Room, but he missed everything else. Because there was no "rest", just immaculate candour. No objects, no people, no shapes.

That he had the wrong room?

No way. So he decided to go back and ask the security man for an explanation.

He turned his back and came upon an unwelcome surprise: the door through which he had entered was no longer there. No cracks in the wall, or any incisions whatsoever, just a completely smooth wall.

The sense of unease grew.

Suddenly she felt himself being pushed from under her legs. Appearing out of nowhere, an armchair emerged from the base of the floor and welcomed him between the armrests. The walls began to colour and shape frames, frames, bookcases. The floor also took on the features of a parquet floor inlaid with asymmetrical figures and a giant central rose window depicting the company logo: a large green star with a hand holding a stylized image of Hire City inside.

A desk took shape in the wall in front of him. In the farthest one, the contours of a door opened, as if a giant knife was sinking into lukewarm butter. Thus appeared the features of a figure.

"The Chief", as everyone called him, liked to get a bit of a show ahead of him when he had to meet a new collaborator. He was the right-hand man of the owner of Soccer Town, Matt Bolsh, and the president of Football H&T Resource. This little show allowed him to achieve two objectives: to amaze and to intimidate. No one had ever seen his face except Bolsh and his faithful. Some argued that they too had never had that privilege.

The most authoritative pens in the major newspapers described him solely on the basis of the wisely sweetened and diffused tissue from the press office in Soccer Town.

The free pens presented him as Mr Mystery. The most accredited voices spoke of three top grades, a wealth of billions of dollars, tons of ambition mixed with unscrupulousness and cynicism, entrepreneurial ability to sell, zero morality. All within a silhouette that would not exceed five feet tall.

Others even denied the existence of the "Chief", suggesting that it was a strategic and publicity stunt by Matt Bolsh.

A skilful crossfire of lights did not allow Torst to peer into the most mysterious face of Hire City, but the figure was that of a man of short stature. At least this rumour seemed to have been confirmed. The not exceptional height, coupled with shapes that widened to a height of 1.20 meters, were the only weak point on which the envious opponents could have leveraged. Perhaps that was why he liked to attack his interlocutors with all that technology.

'Good morning, Detective Torst,' said a friendly hello to the Chief, his voice altered by voice processors.

'Good morning, sir,' replied Torst.

'You may call me Sir Julian. I don't like to keep my distance from my staff. I hope you enjoyed my little display of wonders.'

'Certainly Sir Julian. Never seen anything like it.'

'Recombined matter, my dear. The last devil of the Hire University labs, and of course I'm the only one who owns it.'

'I'd heard about it, but I thought it was just propaganda from the university press office.'

'It's a reality. At last, we can begin to shape the matter as we wish. Too bad that beyond the threshold of four hundred and seventy-five critical units the control is unstable; otherwise I would have already used it for my stadiums. But let's cut to the chase, Torst.'

The register had changed. That little scene had already satisfied his ego sufficiently.

'You must have wondered, I suppose, why I decided to see you after only one hundred and ninety days, six hours and fifty minutes of well-deserved corrupt police work.'

The boss was aware that he was not very delicate in reminding him of his foul play, with one foot in the police and one in the Organization. Torst didn't say a word.

'First of all,' he continued, 'I wanted to meet you to congratulate you. Its efficiency never ceases to surprise me. I knew right from the start I could count on you, the results you've already achieved confirm it.'

'Thank you, Sir Julian,' said the policeman with his mouth full of tension.

'I almost resent having to share you with the Hire City Police. However, I did not summon you just to pay you a few compliments.'

Torst realized that after the pleasantries, it was time for the Chief to get serious.

'What did Katrine Johnson know?' Sir Julian asked point-blank. 'Did you get to talk to anyone before the pickup? I heard she was intercepted at the university.'

'Dr Johnson was unaware of anything and was at the university for personal reasons. I've already given the order to search her villa. Now that the media attention has waned, it will be easier to go unnoticed. The team is ready. Just wait for my signal.'

'Good! I knew you'd do things the best way you could. One last question before I let you go: why did you prefer to suppress the doctor instead of handing her over to the A Team?'

'It was better to give a strong signal.'

'Right!'

'In that regard, may I remind you of my request to join the A-team itself. I could better reconcile my official police duties. At the station they're already starting to get suspicious of my continued absence.'

The boss's look stayed serious. Torst felt intimidated, but he continued.

'I think the work on that team is better planned, I could guarantee myself more effective coverage.'

'Valid argument, Detective Torst. But useless.'

'I don't understand,' replied the policeman.

'Your demands are in vain because as of today you are

already part of that team. Please contact Dr Kafar, he's expecting you at 17:00 in his office to put you on the program immediately.'

Torst breathed a sigh of relief.

'Thank you, sir.'

'Now go, you have work to do. In fact, two,' ironized the chief, who did not repeat the concession to call him "Sir Julian".

'Good day, sir.'

Torst turned and walked out of the opening that had materialized behind him.

Chapter 7

'You've been spreading the word for quite some time, but nothing's happened.'

'Maybe something's moving.'

'You didn't tell me about it. Why?'

'I wanted to make sure it was something concrete and it probably will be.'

'Your friend?'

'No. Looks like two fish took the bait.'

'This could be a trap.'

'Yes, it could. I've also considered that possibility. Before I approach them, I'll do some checking on them. If it's not a face mask, one of them should be a face I know. I'm surprised they managed to get through unscathed, but it's not so impossible otherwise we'd have no hope.'

'One more chance it's a trap.'

'Not necessarily. Some elements make me assume otherwise. I just need a few more hours to do a few more checks and the appointment's the day after tomorrow.'

'From your new position you should have no difficulty.'

'That's right!'

'But be careful not to be too conspicuous. Don't show too much interest in the matter.'

'Take it easy. I'll be careful.'

'You promised to get me out of this hell. You promised me and someone else. Don't forget it.'

'I always keep my promises. I have to go now. A long absence might arouse suspicion. Now is not the time to risk it.'

'Good luck.'

'Drop dead. Get the boys ready, we're close to the big

moment.'
'We're always ready, champ.'
'Until proven otherwise, you are the champion.'
'The others said so.'
'Modest. I have to go now.'
'Fingers crossed.'

CHAPTER 8

Regent Street was located on the outskirts of Block Sixteen, one of seven exclusively residential BBs in Hire City. With a low population density, it was the only one where it was possible to enjoy living architecture.

The counterbalance was a real estate market with dizzying figures, which had to compensate for the very low building concentration and reduced economies of scale.

Regent Street was one of the last crossbars of Harbor Avenue, a vertical axis that divided the Barkley Highs district in two. On both sides, a long line of evergreen maples stood out against the cloud-hemmed sky.

Daniel Keaton's Criton had already travelled the entire circulation space intended for transits and had descended to level A, between zero and ten metres above the ground and intended for free movement.

Once he reached a height of three metres, a splendid Harbor Avenue flaunted its jewels, the most beautiful villas in Hire City.

For the most mischievous and gossipy, and perhaps envious, were only the "spinsters of Harbor Avenue" because they were always alone and constantly on display. The hectic life and commitments of their multimillionaire owners left them uninhabited for most of the year. Nevertheless, having the residence on Harbor Avenue was a must for those who needed to flaunt wealth and power.

The vain parade of old ladies was almost over when the navigator warned to turn right. Daniel agreed to the manoeuvre and soon afterwards he easily recognized Regent Street. He turned off the autopilot and headed for Dr Johnson's villa.

A long avenue led to the imposing building. A laser gate more than ten metres in length preceded it and hologrammed the names of the owners: Konnor & Johnson.

On the right side of the light grille, a monitor flanked an eye scanner that filtered access to the villa by scanning the iris. It was virtually impossible for the unauthorized to access it.

The presence of an eye scanner, if needed, reiterated the strangeness of the gesture made by Dr Johnson: that obsolete microchip card would certainly not help him to penetrate the villa.

'If the woman's last strength was to hand over that card,' he kept saying, 'there must have been a reason.'

Perhaps the card was intended for an alternative entrance to the villa, or a different building.

The map displayed on the navigator indicated the presence of another street – Coeney Street – which flanked the north side of the villa. There was probably a back door right there.

Daniel touched the words COENEY STREET on the on-board holoscreen. His Criton moved by turning right and the navigator pointed to the target fifty metres from the next turn.

His deduction turned out to be correct, and it made him proud: along Coeney Street, the poplars' line was interrupted by a small gate. Once the M-Car had pulled over, he headed towards the new entrance with a loose end, so as not to be conspicuous. In a few seconds, that brilliant intuition turned out to be a new hole in the water.

'Damn!' he whispered quietly by the gate. 'Another eye scanner!'

He looked around annoyed, wondering what else he

could come up with at that point. In the absence of alternatives, and having nothing to lose, he approached the scanner and took a look.

All he could see was a purple light.

An artificial voice made him jump.

'Good morning, sir.'

The gate opened.

The astonishment for the illogical and improbable error of the eye scanner obscured the satisfaction for the small success just obtained. A new riddle had been added to the list, and he no longer paid attention to it. Daniel's hope in this regard was to find all the answers inside the villa.

Once past the gate, a lane opened in front of him, barely one and a half metres wide but at least twenty metres long, which stretched as far as the supposed secondary entrance.

Daniel advanced with rapid pace, escorted by the artificial vegetation that crushed the small path. The route ended with yet another eye scanner placed to guarantee the entrance door.

This time, strengthened by the fortuitous experience of a few seconds before, Daniel immediately offered his iris.

As expected, the door opened. He went in.

Through a small room he had access to a huge hall, which displayed antiques from the twenty-first century in excellent condition. He approached the bookcase that covered the entire north wall to ascertain its authenticity. Although the context was not the most opportune, devotion to everything related to his favourite century had, as always, taken over. It was not possible to deduce, at least from a first and superficial analysis, the actual time of production, but certainly the wood was authentic. The perfume spoke clearly.

Satisfied his curiosity, he moved into the adjacent room,

a hallway from which access to the main entrance and an optiglass open staircase was guaranteed.

The lobby was huge and opulent, emulating the lobby of the best hotels in Hire City. An imposing chandelier hung imperiously in the central area. The walls also had a 21st century style, but were made of iridescent fibre. The decor, on the other hand, was real. At most, it was an excellent reproduction.

Daniel didn't know what to look for or where to look for. He would have liked to be inside those movies where the hero on duty always has the right intuition and knows how to move in every situation. The reality, unfortunately, offered other scripts and he didn't know his scriptwriter.

Having no fixed points from which to begin, he decided to conduct his research in the most sensible way: by probing the structure from the beginning, then from the upper floor and the first room on the left, and then exploring the opposite side and the one below.

Got up the stairs, he took the desired direction. After walking down the long corridor, he approached the first door and opened it. It was the Konnor couple's bedroom. A very normal bedroom, although made of real wood. This time a connoisseur like Daniel couldn't be wrong. A little joke like that was definitely around $2 million, considering the rarity of the material.

For several decades there was no more vegetation except within the protected blocks, where thousands of hectares were reserved for natural forests. Wood had become a good subject for documentaries and school trips, or an opportunity for some multimillionaire to show off his economic power.

No details attracted the attention of Daniel, who did not benefit from reading so many detective novels. He hoped to draw some inspiration from it, but to no avail. He went out.

As he turned left, he noticed a dark corridor in front of him that closed after a few meters. It was totally invisible from the first floor, as it was placed in such a way that it could only be detected from the exit of the bedroom. A half-hidden area and at the same time an architectural imperfection inside a villa where the smallest details were sanctified: it couldn't have been by chance, surely there was something to discover there.

Reinvigorated by that hope, Daniel headed for the blind wall that closed the corridor.

In the other places in the house the automatic lights spread from the walls and accompanied the movements of those who moved inside the villa. In that part, everything stayed in the dark. This circumstance disturbed him. Even as a child, he never loved the darkness.

When he got to the bottom, he stopped. The lights were off. As little as could be seen in the half-light, there seemed to be no other passages or openings.

Convinced more than ever that he would find the answers to his questions right there, Daniel stood still waiting for something to happen.

Nothing.

He started saying words at random.

'Open up!'

Nothing.

'Robert!'

Nothing.

'Katrine!'

Nothing.

He felt the wall to check for cracks, edges or anything else that might be a sensor or control.

Nothing.

Quiet.

From downstairs the cold voice of the artificial responder thundered into the enormity of the central hall.

'*Scanning error. Access denied.*'

Someone was trying to break in through the front door, and they certainly weren't authorized. Daniel deduced from this that he was not the only one interested in Konnor house. It confirms his suspicions once again. If there was something to find out, it had to be right there, in the villa, and unfortunately, it wasn't just him looking for it.

He came out of the darkness, turned right and walked a few meters in the direction of the stairs. A sound blocked it, forcing it back. It was the proverbial four hundred and forty double vibrations. An unmistakable sound for a musicophile like him. It was the most famous note: the La. To play it no instrument, real or virtual of any kind, but the alarm system of the villa.

It was the beep of the sensor confirming access. A second later the artificial voice of the transponder echoed back into the house.

'*Shielding disabled. Access granted.*'

The panel light had changed colour from red to green. Someone would have walked in soon after that.

Passing in front of the main gate, Daniel had been able to calculate the length of the avenue in about fifty metres. The mystery visitor would then take a few seconds to reach the entrance. He had enough time left to get out of the secondary driveway, but a decision had to be made quickly. Alternatively, he could have stayed there, hiding in the dark, and discovered the identity of the second visitor, but running the risk of being discovered.

Events lightened his burden of choice.

A new beep from the entrance resonated in the hall.

Someone was already coming into the house and he wasn't alone anymore.

Surprise. The "mystery visitor" was "the mystery visitors".

A six-man team, armed and equipped with assault suits, had broken into the mansion.

They certainly didn't belong to the police or a known special team.

'Alpha and Bravo, downstairs.'

The arms of what appeared to be the leader pointed to the east side and the west side distributing, in fact, the task to the two.

'November and Charly over the stairs. Tango in the lobby.'

That who gave orders moved around the entrance. He was, perhaps, in charge of covering the avenue or watching other men.

Whoever they were, November and Charly certainly didn't show friendly intentions. They began to climb the stairs and quickly gained the upper floor. It was a matter of seconds. Soon Daniel would know what those gentlemen were up to just to get caught. That mysterious dark recess, along with his dark suit, could offer him a chance for salvation. 'Black on black equals zero contrast at distances greater than one meter,' he said. Some chance of getting away with it still remained. All was not lost.

From his position he could control the first metres of the balcony thanks to the corner mirror. A red string suddenly broke his breath. It was a beam of light coming from the November and Charly's helmet. He knew what it was all about and the odds of staying undercover fell to zero.

'How naive,' he reproached himself. Any military equipment, even the least equipped, required the presence of an infrared viewer. Once past the vestibule, he would be detected and captured immediately. Whether from November or Charly, it didn't really matter.

Daniel felt a growing sense of terror as he pressed his body against the wall even more. Panic was taking over. He turned his palms inwards, almost as if he were smearing himself on the wall. It was as instinctive as it was irrational, a few millimetres more or less couldn't make any difference.

He stood still. His heart was beating so loud that it made a noise, like the *revelatory one* in a very old story.

A few more seconds and he would have known what those guys were up to.

One of the two men was already patrolling the penultimate room, the other had stayed outside to maintain visual control over the field.

A faint light caught Daniel's attention. It came from the portion of the wall he had his hands on. A thin beam of purple light had taken shape and was enveloping it. As he finished his journey, he vanished. The wall began to rotate.

Shortly afterwards he was on the other side.

Darkness.

Quiet.

Chapter 9

'Link activated, Captain.'
'Seconds?'
'Forty-four from now on, before the next opposing scanning.'
'Insertion made but partial. Units are moved to position seven to an unidentified location. Cover the territory and await further instructions.'
'Alpha hypothesis confirmed.'
'We move on to phase two. Green code to all units. Anything new on the recovered subject?'
'None, Captain. The subject is stable, but the clinical picture seems to be improving. Our medical team is doing its best.'
'More communications?'
'Yes, Captain. Regent Street has visitors.'
'Mine?'
'No, Captain. More visits.'
'Have you identified the subject?'
'There's no need for that. He's an acquaintance of ours. It's Daniel Keaton, sir.'
'Put a man on him, but discreetly. Was he carrying anything with him?'
'Apparently not.'
'Damn it!'
'20 seconds to scan, Captain.'
'How did he get in?'
'With the eye scanner, sir.'
'Five seconds.'
'Are they still inside?'
'Affirmative.'
'One second.'
'Over and out.'

Chapter 10

Daniel took a step inward with increasing trepidation. Uncertain, he advanced in the dark. A few metres and the light came on. Step by step. A sort of aurora would light up the room and bring out the contours of the room clearly.

Now the hiding place was well lit. On the left-hand wall there were about thirty monitors, which monitored every corner of the villa.

Monitor number eight captured Mr November and Mr Charly inspecting the first floor. The protagonists of number twelve, fourteen and eighteen were Alfa and Bravo. Channel seven had the guy who was running operations.

After the initial astonishment, Daniel stood staring at the images of the closed circuit. He then noticed, at the bottom of the wall, a console. It was the control panel that handled the puzzle of images transmitted by the security system. The operation was the classic one: on the left side were placed the monitor detectors, on the right side the holographic operator. The monitor and its optical sensor were selected with the left hand. The movement of the right hand, on the other hand, controlled the position and operation of the sensors within the rooms.

All in all, it wasn't hard to use, you just had to get the hang of it.

A few minutes later, monitor number fifteen displayed good news: the military were leaving the villa. The number twenty-one confirmed, recording the final exit of the armed men.

Disposed of the adrenaline produced by that unexpected series of events, Daniel began to take a closer look around.

The hiding place he was in consisted of a single asymmetrical compartment. The array of monitors covered the longest wall. On the opposite side a sofa, two armchairs, a small bookcase. The shelving that housed the books looked like real wood. If it was, it was worth a fortune. The books were authentic, pure 21st century cellulose. It was confirmed by his connoisseur's eye.

Daniel didn't know whether to rejoice at his escape or to have found someone who shared a passion for paper books.

On the shelves of Spartan architecture, like so many showgirls on display and aware of their charm, paraded the most famous titles of the twenty-first and twenty-second century. Among them was his favourite: "The Journey of Harry" by Nicolas Cimino. He'd read it at least 30 times. Over time it had become the manifesto of the noglobals and of all those who fought to denounce the injustices perpetrated by industrialized countries to the detriment of the poorest ones, during the process of global conversion. The copy in the Keatons family library was a reproduction. The one in front of him, most likely, was one of the few original copies left in circulation, worth a few million dollars.

A strip of fine wood separated the upper rows of books from the lower ones. Its width, structure and position could suggest a separating drawer, typical of that style of bookcase. No handle.

Daniel tried to apply pressure with his hand, if there was a rudimentary spring mechanism or a modern hidden sensor. The two hypotheses were almost immediately rejected by failure. No mechanism was triggered.

On the left side of the false drawer a strange inlay caught his attention. It was a more conspicuous carving than the others. He looked inside. A red light dazzled him. Snap back. 'The card,' he thought immediately. It could have been a passkey. Katrine Johnson's extreme gesture made sense.

Daniel went through the pockets of his pants and retrieved the card. He put it right in the slot.

Nothing.

He pulled out the card and checked the sound of it. He put it upside down, but the slot wouldn't accept it. He tried the same way, turning it a hundred and eighty degrees.

Nothing yet.

With his gaze he returned to the monitors to verify that in the meantime the military had not changed their mind and had returned. No sign of danger. The top monitor, however, was relentlessly running a *countdown*.

He ignored when and how it started. He only knew that it had already reached the number forty-one, indicated in red digits.

After a few seconds, something was bound to happen. What?

Thirty-five seconds.

Daniel made an effort to mentally review everything that had happened to him in the last few hours, focusing especially on the last few seconds with Katrine Johnson lying on the ground. In a flash he reviewed the young woman's words when she was still lucid, the grainy eyes of the last moments, the hand that had given him the card, the open palm.

'The open palm!' he thought. 'How could I not think of that before!'

Twenty-nine.

He frantically searched every corner of the library, but without getting any results. Maybe it needed prolonged sensor contact. He then tried to be less hasty and continued to offer the palm of his hand to improbable hidden scanners.

No progress. Meanwhile, the countdown was proceeding relentlessly.

Fifteen seconds.

Daniel thought of a security system that started automatically, one of those that first allows you access and then locks you in like a mouse.

Twelve seconds.

Too late. He walked away and waited standing in front of the far wall for the outcome of the events. He was resigned by now.

Ten seconds.

Perhaps the palm shown by Johnson referred only to the entrance to the room, as he had fortuitously discovered on his own.

Seven seconds.

The countdown numbers had turned blue.

Three.

Two.

One.

A high-pitched hiss accompanied the last number.

Zero.

A message appeared on the monitor.

CHAPTER 11

'Dick Trevor confirmed my appointment.'
'Do you trust me?'
'It doesn't matter.'
'Do you think he really knows him or is that just an excuse?'
'It doesn't matter. We have to go all the way.'
'He came out of nowhere too suddenly, don't you think?'
'We can't ask so many questions.'
'All right.'
'I have to go now. My turn starts soon.'
'Good job and stay alert.'
'Okay.'

Chapter 12

TIMED OPENING
COUNTDOWN COMPLETED

The message closing the countdown disappeared after two seconds.

A click drew Daniel's attention to the library. What looked like a false drawer was a real drawer, and it was opening slowly.

He didn't understand which of his gestures had triggered the mechanism, but the important thing was to have achieved the goal.

With uncertain step he approached. The drawer only contained a older with some papers. He sat in the chair to examine them calmly.

Almost all the documents had the same heading: "Soccer Town Hospital Medical Centre". It was the exclusive medical centre for multimillionaire football players.

The documentation concerned routine clinical examinations, biometric data, reports of microsurgery and cosmetic surgery. Apparently nothing important, at least from an initial analysis.

Only in two documents the header was different. It was the one of Central Hospital in Hire City, the hospital where Dr Johnson worked. So reported the reporter from Hire News.

The first report was compiled by the genetic analysis department. A few lines:

Report: hair.
DNA extraction result: positive and complete.

Matching with FDDB: positive.
Subject: Keaton Daniel - 67, Hamilton Street - Hire City.
Foreign elements detected: elet

At the bottom of the sheet, the paper was ruined and it wasn't possible to read well the last word. The report did not contain a signature, neither manual nor electronic. This absence appeared suspicious to say the least, as it showed that no authorisation had been required for that examination. Daniel hypothesized that Dr Johnson was the head of the department, with free access to the labs and the FDDB, the archive in which all the genetic codes of the inhabitants of Hire City were stored. It was most likely an informal copy, perhaps for internal use. Daniel was surprised, however: that paper had his name on it, and hinted at a test he could never remember taking. He looked for the date on the bottom. He found the one the DNA testers were printing by default:
17:03 - 31 January 2256 - 02904jk1805
The date was prior to their meeting, just two days before. How and why Johnson came into possession of her own hair, he couldn't explain it.

He studied the second report. It had been compiled the day before, in the alphanumeric code only the final number changed:
09:28 - 30 January 2256 - 02904jk1804
The header referred, again, to the genetic analysis department.

Daniel read it carefully.

He didn't believe his own eyes. You read the report again, hoping he misunderstood.

No mistake.

He remembered Dr Johnson's confused words. On that occasion he had interrupted her with bitterness, but with hindsight he reproached himself for having done so: a few more words could be useful to him now and bring him closer to the truth.

The only positive aspect of the story was that he finally managed to understand the reason for the visit and the questions.

He placed the papers in the file and headed towards the part where he had entered. He tried to offer his palm, as he accidentally did to get in, but nothing happened. He then decided to examine the control panel. Surely, the consent for the opening was activated from there.

Activated the OLO command on the console.

The three-dimensional projection of the menus appeared a few inches from his arms. The hands began to explore the command lists. The structure was the classic tree structure.

SAFETY - SENSOR MANAGEMENT - OPENING - MESSAGES were at the first level.

He selected OPENINGS.

On the second level he found: EXTERNAL - INTERNAL - BUNKER.

The bunker was supposed to be the room he was in, so he opted for that command.

At the third level the possibilities proposed by the menu were: OPENING - SETTING. Activated OPEN.

The wall from which he had entered rotated and stopped as a flag. A countdown from number thirty started on the central monitor. The CANCEL command appeared on the right side. He chose it.

Now that he had figured out how to get out, he wanted to calmly continue his exploration inside that hideout to look for some other clue.

He went back through the console levels until he reached MESSAGES. There was only one voice recording in memory.

He selected hit. Waited.

'My love, I think I'm in danger and maybe you are, too...'

The voice was male. It probably belonged to Robert Konnor. The tone was agitated and wheezy. Maybe he was running when he recorded the message. This justified not opting for the holographic version.

'I found out some things about my father and my account. I'd rather not tell you about it, but I can't help it now because you might be involved too. Meet me at home tonight. If I don't make it...'

A rustling replaced the sound of words. Moments after the recording came back clear, but only in flashes:

'...remember... Daniel... I left you a card, it's... remember this name: Daniel.'

The echo of a thud broke the recording. Almost certainly something or someone had blocked it.

Remember this name: Daniel.

The phrase resounded in his head: it was the further confirmation that he was up to his neck in the matter. As for the card, it must have been the card that Katrine Johnson had given him by gathering his last strength.

Daniel tinkered with the commands to display the date of the message: *29 November 2255*. The day Robert Konnor disappeared.

He deactivated the message link, took a last look at the monitors to make sure the road was free of unwanted guests, activated the command to open the bunker. He waited for the moving wall to rotate and once outside he walked backwards along the route taken an hour earlier.

In front of the back entrance he climbed into his Criton. He pulled the stick and the seatbelts wrapped around him. He selected CITY. The vehicle moved.

Someone, a hundred metres behind him, did the same.

CHAPTER 13

Someone was calling him by his name, but in that dark alleyway, there seemed to be no living soul.

'Tony, I'm here!' begged the voice.

Tony was trying to stay calm. That endless running had weighed down his legs. An escape route seemed to surface a few dozen metres ahead. He stared at i and gathered his strength.

'Tony!'

A shadow took the place of the light that had shown him the way out.

Tony stopped.

A face blocked his movements and made his breathing distressing.

'SJ023H... SJ023H...' he repeated almost under hypnosis.

It was him. Finally the voice had a face.

A deaf shot. A cry was swallowed up by silence. The strange figure clung on to Tony's neck with one hand and barely lifted the other trembling. On the palm, in the form of scars, appeared once again the inscription: SJ023H.

With extreme effort he tried to control the trembling of his lips. He opened his mouth to talk, but no sound came out.

'Tony, I did it. We got the signal. Wake up!'

Brandon's voice, but most of all his energetic tugging, woke him up.

He was grateful. He hadn't dreamt for years and starting again with a nightmare hadn't been pleasant.

'Great.' babbled still a little sleepy. He got back on his

feet, reached for Brandon and grabbed the communicator.
'Contact.' scanned with a secure voice.

A beep signalled him that he was unable to execute the command.

'Contact.'

A longer beep confirmed the lack of signal.

'Contact. Damn it!'

The communicator did not give any hint of life, the display started flashing ABSENCE OF SIGNAL.

An eventuality that has been substantially impossible for at least a hundred years, since the entire country was covered by low-altitude bridge satellites.

There were two reasons that could justify such an inconvenience: they were in a shielded area or his five-figure jewel had abandoned him.

The only areas that, for obvious security reasons, the Communications Authority authorised to screen were military areas and government offices of national intelligence.

The likely shielding in Hidden City sounded a little bad. Logically, it had to be a technical fault.

'Contact.'

Nothing.

'I swear the signal was back,' excused Brandon, more sorry for waking him up unnecessarily than for failure itself.

'Contact!'

The tone was tense.

'Give it up Tony, it's not working. We are forced to change our plans,' said his trusty assistant. 'I've also tried the restricted and emergency channels, but everything's in the dark here.'

'I really think Thomas got it right this time too. Too many strange coincidences in Hidden City, and this is just the last one.'

'If I'm honest, the first strange thing about the whole matter is Thomas himself. Did he or did he not give you any directions for the investigation? If we are to consider "clues" a meaningless acronym and a man whose existence you are not even sure of...'

'It's not really like that, Brandon. I've known Thomas too many years not to know that nothing is random or irrelevant to him.'

'You're right about that.'

'After all, we've had confirmation that he is very likely to exist.'

'So what do we do if...'

'First we need to update Thomas on this morning's results. It'll be your job to do it.'

'What about the date? I don't want to leave you alone. I'm not sure about that Dick Trevor. This whole thing doesn't add up, and I've told you several times.'

'I know. I agree with you, but I can go alone. It's important to tell Thomas about the appointment... and everything else.'

Brandon nodded, Tony continued.

'When you get a chance to talk to him, let him know about this sudden communications blackout. He has important friends. They could give us some explanation. Tomorrow you'll leave Hidden City and call Thomas at the first sign in Old Town.'

'They may become suspicious of such a sudden abandonment of office,' remarked the friend.

'I've been thinking about that too. It's not you who leaves, it's them who kick you out. Take these,' he ordered.

'What is it?' Brandon asked anxiously. 'I want to get out of Hidden City on my own two feet.'

'It's not about what you think. It's an alcohol simulator.

You'll only feel your head spin a little bit for the first ten minutes. Tomorrow morning I'm going to snitch and tell the boss that my roommate's having fun. They'll do an instant blood alcohol level test. They'll find enough to kick your ass in less than half an hour.'

Brandon didn't answer. Then, after a deep breath, he swallowed the pills.

Chapter 14

'...which have certainly not yet been erased from the memory of football fans. How not to remember the mythical Hire 404 - Santon Plus of March of two years ago, which ended five to zero for the white-yellow with triplet plus two assists signed "The King". Without delay, in the fifth minute of the first half, Robert Konnor silenced the slanderers that were already relegating him to the players who had started at sunset, despite his young age. Impossible to forget that gallop of eighty meters seasoned with six dribbling plus the final lob of... Damn it! If I'm talking about the dribbling and the lob, you have to show the pictures of that game with the dribbling and the lob! You can't keep dwelling on the opening wheel. I'm not asking so much if I expect you to do your job well. Or do I have to be an editor too?'

'You're right, Thomas, but take it easy. I got a little distracted. We could have corrected the video insertion very well at a later time, without having to stop.'

'Sorry, Matthew. I'm a little nervous today and maybe I shouldn't even have come to the studios.'

Matthew and the second assistant took a look of mutual encouragement. Putting up with the colleague's recent angularity was by no means easy. Shots like this were not part of Thomas' character repertoire, at least until a few weeks earlier.

Everyone in the editorial staff had noticed that something had changed in him recently. The most gossipy people linked the metamorphosis to the absence of news from his right arm, probably engaged in one of their bomb investigations, as usual top secret.

Matthew knew that those conjectures were true and that's

why he didn't mind if his colleague showed all that nervousness in those days. Thomas had confided to him that he was expecting communications by the end of the previous month, but they had never arrived and it was already the 4th February.

Smart-eyed, determination, freckly face, an industrial amount of backwards pulled hair, powerful body, six feet tall, forty-five feet, cowboy attitude. Thomas Lewton, according to many editors, was the most fussy journalist at Hire News, but his fussiness was accompanied by exceptional professionalism and a strong character.

The practice followed by his colleagues was to record the piece in the dark and then leave it to the editors to paste the filmed sequences into it. Thomas, on the other hand, recorded the commentary while the images were scrolling, in order to make the text perfectly adherent to the video and above all to liven up the service with the emotions that the images communicated to him from time to time, so as to be more engaging to the ears of the listeners.

He was Hire News' most watched TV journalist and also the most feared. His investigations-truths had stopped at nothing, not even in front of his superiors, who had sometimes tried to stop him so as not to enter a collision course with the strong powers.

Perhaps also for this reason his career had not followed the paths, paved with successes and awards, beaten by other colleagues, less prone to an incorruptible attitude. All in all, he didn't mind, he was in the trenches wanting to stay. Between people and real facts. He didn't only deal with sports, but with everything that somehow had the ability to arouse his curiosity or his conscience. A nice chair on the 45th floor of the News Building would certainly have bored him.

'Okay. Let's take it from the game reference and then

start with the action pictures.'

'Everything will go smoothly this time,' reassured Matthew, who had positioned himself in front of the console again.

The journalist's communicator vibrated. One glance at the display and his gaze took on a curious air.

'Break, Matthew. We'll resume in 15 minutes.'

In that job, Matthew had been working with Thomas for over five years, so he knew him well. He realized his colleague wanted to be alone and left under the pretext of having coffee.

The journalist accepted the call. There followed a moment of waiting.

'If you came back to ask me for money, you can go to hell,' he said, starting the conversation.

'I called to get back the money you owed me when you ran away, you cheap reporter,' said the other one.

It was the usual good tempered way Thomas and Daniel used to open their chats, the times when they wished to reproach each other for not having been in contact for a long time, taken from work and daily routine.

The friendship between the two of them was foolproof anyway. Born at the time of the oratory, it had always been a strong point of reference for both of them, even though the paths taken subsequently had hindered contacts.

'Hi Thomas, how's it going?' resumed Daniel putting the tone of the interview back on a common track.

'Well, I'd say. What happened? The government extended the day 15 minutes and you found time for friends?'

'Actually...I could use your help.'

The conversation log had changed again. Thomas felt this immediately, and adapted himself.

'What's going on, Daniel? Don't make me worry about

you too.'

'I need to talk to you immediately. I'm already on my way. Where are you?'

Out of place to ask if the meeting was important or urgent. It had to be something serious.

'I'm at the News Building. I'll meet you at the parking lot entrance in ten minutes.'

'Well, I'll be there,' concluded his friend.

Thomas gave instructions to the secretary to move all appointments for the day and to inform Matthew that the recording session was cancelled. He'd be in touch as soon as he could.

He took the green jacket from the coat rack, walked down the long corridor that separated him from the reception, slipped into the panoramic lift and pressed the T button.

The Panoramic Lift covered the entire height of the News Building, a complex of three million four hundred thousand square metres scientifically distributed over two hundred and thirty-four floors. A city within a city, an immense cigar with iridescent external walls, made from a forty-five centimetre layer of optiglass, a special material with a transparent appearance like glass but containing programmable fibres.

Its external peel was used both for advertising purposes and to change the appearance of the building. Cigar liked to get a new look every once in a while. Famous is the time when cyber-stylers turned it into a majestic aquarium. The typical aspect, however, was the transparency of the walls in order not to hide the ten thousand employees who, like ants, moved neatly inside.

Regardless of the proposed artistic solution, the News Building stood out above all for its characteristic roof: here a fifty-metre obelisk, which supported the N and B visible from any corner of the city, was attacked by a forest of antennas, satellite dishes and bridges.

The scenic lift was going fast. On each floor you could see aseptic rooms covered with computers and swarming with journalists, photographers, editors-in-chief, *anchorman*, operators. Every fifteen floors a level was dedicated to both physical and mental refreshment: canteen, bar, cinema, reading rooms, massage rooms, swimming pools and saunas.

Already at the height of the 120th floor you could see Daniel's Criton on the Big Gate. It was moving fast. It'd be here in seconds.

Chapter 15

'The date's tonight.'
'Did they take the bait?'
'Yes.'
'Have you thought of everything?'
'Dick Trevor's a precise guy, you should know that.'
'Now go.'

Chapter 16

The panoramic lift immediately reached the ground floor. The doors of that crystal box lowered and disappeared, leaving room for the exit.

Just outside, Thomas used the treadmill that would lead him to the parking lot.

The News Building was specially built on the edge of the Block, near the parking spaces: a fundamental requirement for journalists, who had to be always ready to attack the news.

It would have taken just 3 minutes and 27 seconds. He had already timed it several times.

Thomas took that time to organize the lecture he was going to give to his friend for his long time on the run. Then he thought the same accusation could be made against him. He decided, therefore, to give up. They hadn't had a good reunion for months.

The treadmill unloaded him at exit number eighteen. Daniel was already there waiting for him.

'Get in.'

'Yes, sir!'

Thomas took his place on the Criton. He added, 'It must be really serious, if you didn't go to the university today and decided to look up an old friend.'

'I took a couple of days off. My nerves are in tatters. More things have happened to me in the last few hours than in the last 30 years.'

'I sensed the importance of the matter. What's going on?'

Daniel didn't answer. His face was pulled. He tinkered with the on-board computer and selected AUTO.

The windows of the Criton darkened and the two friends were pushed slightly into the seats. They were getting up to the exit level.

The professor broke the silence.

'Do you know Robert Konnor?'

'Of course I know him. I mean, I know who he is, but I've never met him personally.'

'What can you tell me about him?'

'A lot of things, I've often dealt with his exploits. When you called me, I was editing a report on a game that Konnor was in, by the way. The five-zero trimmed to those of Santon Plus. He played great. But what have you got to do with Robert Konnor?'

'Yesterday morning, in my studio at the university, Katrine Johnson showed up. I think you know who we're talking about.'

'Konnor's wife. She committed suicide just yesterday.'

'It wasn't suicide.'

'How do you know that?'

Daniel started spilling his guts. To the concrete need to inform him of the facts was added the need to share that burden.

Thomas listened to everything in respectful silence. He only spoke at the end.

'The important thing, to begin with, is to understand why Dr Johnson went looking for you.'

'I found out in the bunker,' replied Daniel, giving his friend the documents he had brought with him. The journalist grabbed them and went through them.

'What kind of trouble are you in?' he asked after reading.

'I had never met that woman before yesterday morning and I was completely ignorant of her existence.'

'So the reports are fake?'

'No, I don't think that. It wouldn't make sense.'

'They look authentic,' confirmed Thomas. 'Dr Johnson falsifying reports and then coming back to ask you... No, it doesn't make sense. The second report is incredible.'

'It's more plausible that she was using the reports to frame me.'

'The reason?'

'I don't know. Certainly not for money, she didn't miss them.'

'If she had no ambition and the reports are authentic, we'll just have to ask a few questions at Central Hospital. We have a friend right in the genetics department. Am I right?' asked Thomas with a wink.

Daniel tried to put it back on a less uncomfortable track.

'The foreign substance detected on my hair is illegible. Do you know something that starts with *elet*?'

'I'm neither a chemist nor a doctor. I repeat, however, a friend of ours works at Central Hospital.'

Attempting to deflect that speech had failed. Might as well face it head-on.

'You, if anything, have a friend in the genetics department,' Daniel pointed out.

'Stop it! Again with this? My goodness, it's been years!'

Daniel realized he had gone too far.

'Sorry, you're right,' he admitted then.

'Like it or not, we need her today. If we ask too many questions, it might arouse suspicion. We still don't know what happened and especially who we can trust. She's still our number four.'

'At your age you still think that shit?'

'It ain't bullshit oaths between friends.'

'You're talking about things that happened 30 years ago. Do you realize that?'

Thomas thought about it for a moment.

'For me, they remain serious things...' he admitted with candour.

'So serious that at the first opportunity someone went their own way, and you know who I mean.'

'In his place you would have done the same.'

'It's not true,' cut Daniel short. 'I would have kept my end of the bargain. Anyway, I don't think this is the time to go back to that kind of talk. I asked for your help, not a lecture.'

'Then let's head over to Central Hospital, to Josie. She's waiting for me there. She's on day shift.'

'Have you heard from each other?'

'Yes, yesterday. I told her I was going to see her today. I've wanted to talk to you about Jerry for a couple of days. I was hesitant whether to do it with you. Fortunately, your call dispelled the doubt.'

Daniel reactivated the on board computer, allowing the Criton to slow down.

'Central Hospital.' he ordered.

The voice sensor took the command. On the screen the word ACTIVE appeared. The Criton resumed speed.

'What does Jerry want from you? An interview?' filmed Daniel in a polemical tone. 'Does he want to make up for lost headlines? Or does he want to give you one of the girls they stuck him with as a severance package?'

'Jerry is in danger,' said Thomas lapidary.

'Is he tired of having a good time from morning till night?'

'I'm serious. I have reason to believe that Jerry is in grave danger.'

'How do you know that?'

'I've come to know something about us.'

Thomas hesitated. He seemed to fear his friend's reaction, but he was determined to play the wild card right away. It was the only way to get his attention.

'Meaning what?' Daniel pushed him.

Thomas made up his mind.

'What if I told you SJ023H?'

Daniel's face went dark.

CHAPTER 17

'He's on his way to Central Hospital, sir.'
'Is he alone?'
'No, sir. He is in the company of another subject.'
'Have you identified him?'
'Thomas Lewton.'
'The journalist?'
'Affirmative.'
'Keep me posted.'
'It will be done, sir.'
'Hidden City?'
'We're almost ready and it looks like something's moving.'
'Fine.'
'Over and out.'

Chapter 18

'I see you have a good memory,' said Daniel trying to hide the tension. That short alphanumeric series upset him.

'If remembering six figures means having a good memory, yours isn't bad either,' Thomas replied, implying that his instinctive reaction had not escaped him, even though he had skilfully tried to hide it.

'Do you still remember that nonsense?' continued Daniel sarcastically.

'That code is not stupid. You know it.'

'It would only be serious if it hadn't been only thirty-five years. Does that sound like something to overlook?'

'No. It's not a detail to overlook, but we have a duty to make sure nothing bad has happened to Jerry. That's why I wanted to talk to you and Josie about it. It is our oath.'

'Again with this oath. We were kids," slammed impatient Daniel. 'I understand that a little nostalgia is always good, but from here to...'

'If you really thought that way, you wouldn't have that reaction,' Thomas said. 'Throw away, at least once in your life, that armour you always wear.'

He hit the nail on the head. Daniel wasn't replicating, and that was a good sign. He went on.

'The combinations of twenty-six letters plus ten numbers, in a six-digit code, are more than two billion. It's virtually impossible for anyone to think of the same sequence. Remember?'

Daniel remained impassive.

'Am I mistaken or are those your words, Professor Daniel Keaton?'

'Thirty-five years ago, Thomas. Thirty-five years ago,' he replied in an almost obsessive tone. 'I understand that being a journalist makes you see complicated plots even when they're linear, but this time you've really outdone yourself.'

Daniel seemed to have woken up from that sort of mental catalepsy.

'Haven't you thought about the possibility, much simpler and more plausible, that he might have told someone?' he added in a dizzyingly loud voice. 'To a friend, to one of his hundred thousand girls, to his psychoanalyst. Have you considered the possibility that maybe he wants to play a prank on us and ridicule us? Keep your feet on the ground, Thomas. Don't you start to tell storie about a guy who hasn't been in touch with you or Josie for years because he's too busy getting his ass massaged and showing off his idleness at other people's expense.'

'Jerry would never do that. We all swore it,' Thomas shot.

'We also took another oath, and it seems to me that Jerry broke it. Doesn't your shining memory remember this particular one?'

The tone was back to sarcastic.

'We've talked about this many times and you know how I feel.'

'It doesn't matter what you think, or what he invented afterwards. The facts count, and that is that he accepted despite the oath.'

'All right, but let's focus on the present. I'm telling you again that Jerry is in danger,' Thomas resumed. 'There are some details I haven't told you about yet.'

'They would be?'

'First, there's a man who calls himself SJ023H...'

'And you're telling me this now?'

'Sure, so in the meantime you could look like an idiot

who still lives in the past.'

Daniel preferred not to argue, on the other hand, he had done the figure of the idiot seriously. He just asked,

'What do you mean when you say "he calls himself"?'

'It's the code name he uses in his...environment. Once I heard this news, I momentarily stifled my pride and got in touch with Jerry at Football Eden.'

'Result?'

'No one. It was practically impossible to talk to him. A rubber wall everywhere. They glanced with all kinds of excuses: 'we have to protect privacy,' 'we can't talk to journalists,' 'we're not allowed to put you in touch with Mr Crenna."

The light signal from the on board computer interrupted the conversation. The countdown was 53 seconds. In less than a minute they would have arrived at their destination. The Criton decelerated sharply. The display indicated the descent area. The windows became transparent again.

Thomas' communicator vibrated and, after consent, a small image took shape.

It was the face of a man in his 40s.

'Hello, genius,' greeted Thomas. 'I've been looking forward to your call. Do you have something for me?'

'You were right. There are too many details that I'm not convinced of and I'd like to talk to you about them.'

'Where are you now?'

'In my studio.'

'I'll be with you in 20 minutes. Wait for me.'

'All right. See you in a bit.'

The image of the interlocutor was sucked by the communicator.

'What does it mean "I'll be with you in 20 minutes"? Have you forgotten the appointment with Josie?'

'You go to Josie, explain the situation to her and do your research. Head to the taxi zone, please.'

Daniel grabbed the stick and the sign AUTO disappeared from the display. He turned right.

'What's on your mind?' he asked, staring straight ahead.

'I asked a friend to look at some footage. I have a theory and I want to test it.'

'What theory are you talking about?'

'These are videos about Jerry. I'll tell you about it as soon as I've checked a few things out. Have you ever heard of Maurice Billom?'

'The name rings a bell, but right now I can't connect it to anyone in particular.'

'We are talking about one of the most important sports journalists, as well as an excellent editor and videographer. He's very well known in journalism. He has a degree in biometric engineering. A few days ago I gave him a couple of videos to look at. I'm on my way to see him. I think it might help you too, on the Robert Konnor thing. He knows everything about everybody. It's a real encyclopaedia.'

Daniel received the information without responding.

The Criton had already stopped in front of the taxi stand and waited for instructions.

Thomas put his hand near the door, which opened and disappeared laterally. He went down.

'As soon as you've spoken to Josie, join me in Soccer Town.'

'Okay.'

'I forgot...' added Thomas. 'Josie just broke up with her boyfriend.'

For a moment, a smile of satisfaction appeared on Daniel's face.

It disappeared just as quickly.

CHAPTER 19

'We have a problem in Hidden City.'
'What kind?'
'Two unwelcome guests.'
'Did they find anything?'
'No. Not yet at least, but they ask too many questions. They're looking for one in particular.'
'You find him first.'
'You're damn right. As a precaution, we cordoned off the area a few days ago.'
'Well done.'
'Are they both under your control?'
'One of them got himself kicked out, but we're keeping an eye on him.'
'The other one?'
'It's Tony Stantford.'
'Listen up. Here's what I need you to do...'

Chapter 20

Tony Stantford was Thomas Lewton's operating arm.
Two full marks in Journalism and Literature of the 21st century. Karate black belt. Slim body, one metre and sixty-five, hair shaved at the sides and short at the front. Round face, black eyes, thin eyebrows. Variable clothing or, as he specified, camouflage. He loved to blend in with the environment to explore. If he had to take care of an investigation at the Hire City Stock Exchange, he'd pull out his grey pinstripes. If he had to write a piece about youthful discomfort and new electro drugs, then he dusted off his old rebellious young man's clothes from the closet, hoping to get into them again every time.

Thomas' companion of a thousand adventures, they had brought home the hottest investigations in years. They had become famous thanks to the mythical report generally indicated by their surnames, Lewton-Stantford, a reportage whose echo had hit the then Governor Simon Malcom. The high official had played dirty with two cards: on the one hand, he had favoured the promulgation of laws prohibiting experiments on human cloning, on the other he had secretly financed secret laboratories that were dealing with cloning in order to develop an autonomous replication protocol.

The scandal report was followed by the investigation of the magistrates and then numerous arrests, including that of the chief of staff for scientific research, a dozen scientists and some corrupt policemen from the health control unit.

The only one who escaped capture was Simon Malcolm. He jumped into the Himming River a few seconds before the National Guard's unwelcome visit and was never found.

The police had reason to believe the death of the politician, given the height of the launch and the prohibitive conditions in Himming.

The investigation brought a lot of notoriety and prestige to the two of them, especially to Thomas Lewton, who was more exposed from the media point of view.

Success and fame, however, were also an obstacle to subsequent investigations. Known throughout the state, Thomas' face had become too well known to go unnoticed. It was from then on that he began to manage his investigations mainly from behind the scenes, availing himself of the precious collaboration of Tony and Brandon who, skilfully remaining in the semi-darkness of the media, could move undisturbed and without being too noticed.

The new investigation that Tony was following with Brandon, under Thomas' omnipresent supervision and cooperation, concerned Hidden City.

Ghetto neighbourhood of Old Town, Hidden City was now the only refuge for tramps and outcasts in various capacities. The only law that existed down there was that of survival, often to the detriment of the weakest. The surveillance service was watching, the important thing was not to disturb the peace of the rest of the city and that everyone stayed in their place. Thanks to an influential friend, Tony and Brandon had infiltrated the security forces to investigate the alleged construction of a barrier that would prevent the people of Hidden City from crossing the borders and pouring into the sorrounding neighbourhoods.

The two reporters' investigation had taken a particular turn when Tony learned of a bum who called himself SJ023H. He had judged that name to be a detail of colour, capable of enriching the journalistic piece he was working on. He had talked to Thomas about it and his friend's reaction had turned out to be rather anomalous. He immediately demanded more information about the man. Tony didn't have the courage to ask why.

In the days that followed, Tony and Brandon's investigative work had focused on finding the homeless man with the eccentric name. The first step was to go back to the bar where Tony met the guy who told him about SJ023H.

Five attempts had failed. Then Tony was approached by a colleague, Dick Trevor, who had recently been hired by the security team number seventy-three. He said he heard he was looking for a homeless guy with a weird name and that he could help him. One of his informants was supposed to point him to the exact place to find him the next day.

The sudden appearance of Dick Trevor had aroused some suspicion in Brandon and Tony, but the two didn't feel like abandoning the only available lead and letting slip a faint hint. 'You have to take a risk,' they thought.

The mission involved great danger and that's why Tony wanted to remove Brandon under the pretext of warning Thomas. The absence of connections and the consequent isolation, besides worrying him, had given him the excuse to get him out of that situation.

Brandon took the bait. Not because he was stupid, but because of the extreme trust that bound him to his friend.

Chapter 21

'Good morning. Dr Josie Smith, please.'
The receptionist raised her eyebrows to salute him back.
'Who wants her?'
'Daniel Keaton.'
'Just a moment.'
The girl started fiddling with the console.
'Dr Smith will be with you in ten minutes. In the meantime, you can take a seat in the waiting room,' the receptionist said, indicating the adjacent room.
Daniel moved in next door.
His breathing was slow and measured. He was trying to control his emotions. Seeing her again after so long couldn't leave him indifferent.
Daniel and Josie's friendship had distant roots. She was born in the oratory of Father George, an authentic white fly fighting to enhance human relationships in a world dominated by the virtual.
The two kids were only half of a quartet known to their peers as "The Musketeers". Jerry and Thomas were part of it, too.
The name came to Daniel. In his father's library he had discovered a 19th century book by a certain Dumas, entitled "The Three Musketeers". He had read it with greed and was impressed by the bond between the protagonists of the novel.
Daniel and Jerry were also champions of the neighbourhood football team. Two phenomena. Of the two, though, Daniel was the best. The phenomenon of phenomena.
Star of the small championship of the "Very Young", true

volcano of fantasy, annihilated his opponents with drunken dribbling. The football flair of the little tightrope walker would have surprised even the inventiveness of the best sports game programmer.

Not even Jerry, five years older than Daniel, joked with his feet and on several occasions risked taking the scene away from his friend.

Thomas, on the other hand, dribbled better with words and was by now fully entitled to be Father George's right-hand man in his battle against the "evils of the modern world", as he called them. Despite his young age, he had put him in charge of his independent newspaper, "The Contact".

Josie had begun to attend the oratory as the only way to approach Daniel, for whom she had a particular attraction. It was immediately pure empathy, even with Jerry and Thomas. The trio soon turned into a quartet, just like in Dumas' novel. Hence the idea of the name.

The camaraderie of the four guys acquired strength and quality over time. "The carabiners", as Father George called them when he wanted to spite them, were his flagship, the best result of the life mission he was fighting for.

Daniel's fantasy emerged not only in the game of football, but also in the life of the group. He had gone out of his way to invent the "algorithmic names", the "talking fingers" and the "rescue code".

The "algorithmic names" were the fancy names that the four friends used to call themselves to be sure of their identity, in messages and voice communications. The aim was to avoid the jokes of the other boys in the oratory, envious of the bond that the four had cemented. Daniel had created a simple algorithm by which he determined the name to be given. The parameters taken into account were the number of the day and month in which they were located and the weather conditions on the previous day. An infallible and easy to remember system.

The "talking fingers" were a non-verbal communication system. To each letter of the alphabet Daniel had associated a specific position of the five fingers, a bit like in the language of the deaf-mute. An ingenious system that so many times had allowed the four to tear the rivals apart in the games organized by Father George.

The "rescue code", on the other hand, was a six-digit alphanumeric code, drawn by lot with a simple random operation. A code to use as a last chance in case of serious danger. The stunt had earned Daniel a lot of teasing from his friends, but he was stubborn in defending the idea and its usefulness. It had set up a random selection operation on the hand held from twenty-six letters of the alphabet plus ten numeric digits, in order to create a combination of six elements. The monitor had spit out SJ023H.

In the end, the friends had ended up indulging him and inserting the code into the text of their oath, which they recited when they met to talk about important things.

On February 2, 2227, Soccer Town entered Daniel's life.

Matt Bolsh's efficient money grinding machine was always on the lookout for talent among local clubs, especially young ones. Even the parish teams weren't spared. The imperative was precise: 'if there is a champion, we must find and capitalize on him'.

Finding a talent involved figures with several zeros. Those who let themselves be swallowed up by football had an almost compulsive need for new faces, new stories, new tightrope walking feats. If then the talent found was at most fourteen years old, then the "phenomenon" was built, preciously decorated by the media wave and skilfully packaged by the

Image Division of Soccer Town.

The families of the selected ones were persuaded to allow their children to enter the temple of football with dizzying figures, useful to reward them for the very high risk that the boys ran: burning their future.

Only a few were able to reach the top and the big earnings promised. Many, on the other hand, were lost in the streets or remained anonymous after giving up a normal life to chase evanescent dreams of glory.

That day, the headhunters from Soccer Town came to Father George's oratory. Perhaps the fame of the two phenomena had reached them.

Their visit didn't last long, just the time to exchange a few words with the coach, Father Jeff, during the training match. Sometimes they looked up to the playing field, but it seemed like they already had a clear idea of what they were looking for.

At the end of the game the coach didn't even wait for Daniel and Jerry to return to the locker room. 'They were here for you two. Do you know who they are?' he asked them. The two friends had sensed something and those simple words confirmed everything.

Now that Father Jeff had made Soccer Town's interest official, they couldn't wait.

The first hours of euphoria were followed by days of anxiety, waiting for their parents to decide whether or not to accept the Soccer Scouts' offer. The two boys, in their last four-way meeting, swore allegiance to each other: if one of them did not obtain consent from their parents, the other would refuse the offer.

Fate put them to the test. The Crennas family, Jerry's family, gave their consent. William Keaton, on the other hand, aided by the financial strength of his family, refused despite repeated upward offers.

Daniel's dreams turned into nightmares. It seemed to him that all of a sudden life had imploded in his heart. The fights with the father were bitter, but no useful results were obtained. The world collapsed on him. The explanations given by the father focused on the ephemeral side of the football career, on the risk of being dazzled by sequins and losing touch with reality.

Nothing could ease the boy's pain, not even the intercession of Father Jeff who, despite agreeing with William Keaton, proposed more blunt but equally unproductive arguments about him and his torment.

The only result Daniel achieved was punishment. He was segregated in the house for a month.

On his return to the oratory, a similar pain awaited him: Jerry had not kept his oath and had accepted the Soccer Scouts' proposal.

From that moment on Daniel removed the football, and everything that revolved around it, from his own life. He drowned his thoughts in his second vocation: books and study.

Soon the fates of the *four musketeers* took different directions. Daniel's followed the path of his university career. Jerry, as expected, became a football star. His talent allowed him to stay on the crest of the wave for a long time, only to end his golden life in Soccer Eden, the paradise reserved for footballers at the end of their sporting careers. Thomas was quick to point out his literary skills and burned through all the stages of his journalistic career, going directly from "The Contact" to the largest newspaper in the state, Hire News. His affection for Father George, however, never waned; he continued to write free for his first paper, and to support it in a thousand ways. Josie went to medical school.

After the initial isolation, Daniel slowly resumed relations with Thomas and Josie. With the latter he met again at university, an environment in which their friendship turned into love. Daniel's courtship was long and romantic, hampered by Josie's initial perplexities about the risk of debasing or destroying a friendship found after so long. Daniel's tenacity, the moments stolen from the study, the long walks on campus, made her capitulate.

The magical moment came true for her birthday, celebrated in the best restaurant in the university city. During dinner Daniel had her bring a white and yellow iridescent fibre orchid that after a few seconds, becoming transparent, let a ring of brilliants emerge inside.

The message was explicit and required a response.

The answer was yes.

The idyll lasted only a year, the time to finish the preparatory courses together. Having opted for different degree courses, their destinies separated again.

They agreed to give priority to their respective careers and to keep intact the friendship that united them, and that too hastily had been reshaped into something else.

Daniel became a hardened single man. A few years later, he learned that Josie had got engaged to her cell mutation professor. That's also why he didn't look for her anymore.

The merry-go-round of memories was interrupted by a voice.

'Good morning, Professor Keaton.'

A female figure had appeared at the waiting room door. That was Josie.

Chapter 22

If he met her by chance, he might have had a hard time recognizing her. No more than a second, anyway. The voice hadn't changed.

The white coat hid the graces of the body but not those of a face of refined beauty, enriched by an elegant expression.

Josie was casually wearing her 40s. Straight hair, blond with a jaunty cut. Dry face embellished with deep intelligent emerald green eyes. Pale complexion. One and seventy-eight tall, confident air and proud looks. She had been working in the genetics department for nine years and enjoyed a respectable reputation in the medical world because of her research. She'd been single for a few weeks.

Daniel greeted her in the neutral tone he used when he wanted to hide his embarrassment.

'Actually, I was expecting a visit from Thomas today,' she said. 'Better that way. I'm very happy to see you again.'

Daniel appreciated the larification.

'Really?'

She smiled to calm him down.

'I'll have to mark this day on the calendar, meeting both you and Thomas is rare. By the way, he should be here any minute.'

'Thomas is not coming. We were together until a few minutes ago, but he had to run off somewhere else. He asked me to talk to you about some things. Not here, of course.'

'Sure,' Josie reassured him. 'Let's go to my studio.'

They walked down the corridor, at the end of which there was a service lift reserved for doctors. Josie put her hand on the bridge. The doors opened and the two entered.

'Have you come to return a favour to Thomas, then?' Josie asked as the lift was moving down.

'Not only that. I need your help with a problem that concerns me.'

'Then I welcome the trouble.'

They both smiled, entrenched behind a silence full of meaning.

Once in her studio, Josie asked her old friend how she could make herself useful. Daniel handed her the documents from the bunker.

'These reports are from Central Hospital. They're from this very ward. Can you tell me more about them?'

Josie read everything calmly, lingering over the second report. She looked up.

'It's not what you think,' Daniel immediately said to nip his friend's comments in the bud. 'If they were true, I wouldn't be here asking for your help.'

A second later, Daniel realized he'd made a mistake. It was unkind to point out the opportunistic purpose of his visit.

'I mean,' he tried to recover, 'we wouldn't be here to talk about these reports. Maybe something else.'

Josie played dumb.

'They're informal prints.'

'Can you tell me who made these?'

'Sure. I can trace the clock number back to the user who had access to the analyser at the time.'

'Can you do it now?'

'I'm already doing it.'

Josie sat at her desk and moved her hands over the keyboard. A beep signaled the rapid arrival of the result.

'What have you got to do with Johnson?' Josie asked.

'Good question. Nothing, at least until yesterday morning.'

Daniel made her friend share in all his vicissitudes. Josie, after listening carefully, proposed her interpretation of the facts.

'The analysing machine is not manipulable. The only alteration could have occurred upstream on the artefacts analysed.'

'What about the unknown substance you can't read, can you tell me about it?'

'It's definitely some artificial compound, because there's no natural element that starts with those letters. Let me check.'

Josie's hands returned to the keyboard and the computer provided the result. That's what she thought.

'There are over two thousand five hundred substances registered in the archive beginning with "elet". It's like looking for a needle in a haystack. Anything I said to you, I'd guess.'

She checked the time.

'Now there's too many people in the lab and too many eyes,' she snorted, grabbing his communicator. She activated it. 'This is Dr Smith. I need to book the diagnostic room for some confidential tests.'

A moment of silence.

'At 19:00 is fine. Thank you.'

Daniel waited.

'I can verify the authenticity of the finds and redo the analysis. It's the only way I can help you,' Josie specified. 'I'm not promising you anything good. Don't kid yourself. It's likely that the organic find was never filed away.'

'I've considered that possibility.'

'I hope to find something in the Analyser's memory. Maybe we can read the whole report. That would already be an achievement.'

'Okay. Thank you. Now I have to get to...'

'There were two things you needed to talk to me about or do I remember wrong?' Josie interrupted him.

'Yes. Trouble never really comes alone. As if my troubles were not enough, I must also indulge Thomas and his delusions.'

'Meaning?'

Daniel didn't go around it.

'Thomas is convinced that Jerry is in danger. A man called SJ023H has come to our attention.'

'Our SJ023H?'

The deep green eyes harboured the nostalgia for that magical period of their existence, then overcome by age and the inexorable laws of everyday life.

'When you have a chance in over two billion combinations, whose do you want it to be?' he remarked.

'What's your idea? Do you really think Thomas's are fixations?'

Josie had not lost her extraordinary ability to read people's souls.

'I think Jerry's in danger of getting bored because he's made too much money over the years, and told someone about our teenage nonsense.'

'It still burns you after all this time, doesn't it?'

Daniel preferred to avoid the subject.

'This time I really have to go. Thomas is waiting for me. I'll leave you my number, so as soon as you have any news, we can talk.'

'I already have it,' Josie boldly admitted. 'I asked Thomas a few weeks ago because I wanted to call you, but then I didn't.'

Daniel would have wanted to ask why, but Josie's eyes

looked sufficiently eloquent.

'Good. Then we'll stay in touch.'

'Say hi to Thomas for me, please.'

'It will be done.'

Daniel headed toward the elevator, offering his back to his friend. He went in. The mirror on the opposite wall revealed Josie's gaze fixed on him.

He brought the palm of his hand closer to the sensor. The doors closed.

CHAPTER 23

'I have learned to my great regret that there is too much activity in Hidden City.'

'You're right, Sir Julian.'

The man's voice vibrated irregularly. He was scared.

'You assured me that certain out-of-programme people would no longer entertain us. Am I wrong?'

Sarcasm blatantly joined the threat.

'We're having trouble locating them. They probably haven't found a location shielded or uncovered by our detectors. It's the only plausible explanation. If we're lucky enough to locate...'

'There is no such thing as luck for Julian Preston! There is only efficiency, Mr Jewa, and I will not tolerate billions of dollars going up in smoke because of the incompetence of my men.'

The Chief stood up and gestured on his console. Although he had changed his position, even from that angle the clever play of light continued to hide his face.

'We already have a lead to follow. We're also exploiting the unfortunate intrusion of those two. Believe me, sir, it's the best we could do. We're keeping the situation under control.'

'I created the impossible in my life and I'm not willing to let a handful of derelicts step on my toes.'

Jewa tried to remain calm, but trembled at the idea of verifying the conjectures that hovered over the fate of those who, unfortunately, had tasted the wrath of that man. Those directly concerned, moreover, had never been able to report anything, having disappeared into thin air.

His fears came to life.

From the wall behind, two mechanical arms materialized and grabbed his throat. Jewa squinted his eyes and immediately tried to free himself, but the pressure exerted on his neck was too strong and his attempts were worthless.

The breath became difficult, small cyanotic patches began to appear on the face. The grip allowed him to breathe just enough to keep him conscious, but it was tight enough to make him wish he were dead.

Julian Preston got out of his cage of lights and took a few steps forward. Now the part above the neck was visible.

Lawrence Jewa recognized that face.

Preston noticed. Besides, that's exactly what he wanted. To reveal his identity was the gift for his condemned prisoners, a macabre and narcissistic practice that he loved to repeat to exalt the ego, the times when he was called to eliminate a disappointing collaborator.

'I note with pleasure that my face is not new to you. I can give you good news and bad news, then. Which do you prefer first?'

The delirium of omnipotence intoxicated him and therefore prolonged the torment of the condemned man on duty.

'All right, I'll decide. I'll give you the good one first.'

Jewa's eyes, filled with terror, stood still.

'The good news is you can also call me Simon Malcolm. It's a privilege I grant to a few. The bad news is I don't give it for long, so I'm forced to kill you.'

The hands of recombined matter carried out their cruel mission of death. Jewa didn't even have the strength to scream.

After allowing a glimpse of the lifeless body of the man, Simon Malcolm was satisfied. He walked away with his sneer and the life of his former collaborator.

Chapter 24

It was getting late.

Dick Trevor hadn't shown up yet. Tony had been sitting at the table sipping his pear juice for over three hours.

Even though he was nursing the drink, he had already reached the fourth glass. He decided that would be the last one. Brandon's lack of news worried him, so he would have missed the appointment gladly.

As planned, that morning Tony had faked a tip about his friend's alleged hangover, who had been kicked out immediately after blood tests. In his plans, Brandon should have been out of Hidden City by now to make contact with Thomas and return with reinforcements. He hoped everything went smoothly, but his sixth sense said something else.

Like every day, Tony took off from his undercover work at 15:00 in the afternoon. He was on the first shift. After having a bite to eat, he fell asleep on the couch, so he immediately joined the evening in the afternoon. Around 18:30 he went to the bar where he had an appointment with his colleague. Not a shadow of him, until then.

A few more sips of hope and then he would have accepted failure. The waiter approached to remove the glass.

'Do you need another juice?' the young man asked.

'No, thank you. I'm leaving,' replied Tony.

A voice interrupted them.

'The gentleman will have another drink. For me the same.'

That was Dick Trevor. Tony stayed in his seat and beckoned him to sit down. The colleague accepted the invitation.

'Sorry I'm late, but force majeure got in the way,' Trevor

said.

'I see.'

Tony adjusted to the chair and stared at his interlocutor.

'Have you heard where we can find our man?'

'Sure. In a place about ten kilometres from here.'

Meanwhile, the waiter had served two juices.

'Don't tell me a guy like you drinks pear juice! If I had sensed it, I would never have ordered the same thing,' Trevor said surprised.

'Never order in the dark,' Tony replied.

Dick Trevor resumed again.

'There's a meeting of tramps scheduled, the guy will definitely attend. The meeting is in an hour, we have plenty of time to enjoy your dangerous drink and get to the place. I've got some rags in my scooter, we'd better put them on if we don't want to be discreet, those guys are very suspicious and chaste.'

'Fine.'

'Tell me about your man,' continued Trevor. 'Why are you looking for him?'

'Pure journalistic curiosity.'

Tony remained cautious towards his colleague. That sudden interest aroused suspicion. He decided, therefore, to stay as buttoned up as possible.

'You're a journalist, then?' replied Trevor.

In the need not to reveal anything about SJ023H's identity, he had lowered his guard on his own. A beginner's mistake, which he remedied immediately.

'Unfortunately, I'm not. That would be my dream. Sometimes I send freelance services to Hire News to raise some money. I heard about that homeless guy with the weird name, so I thought I could get a piece of colour and maybe make a few bucks on it.'

From the appearances it seemed that the colleague had drunk the excuse and that the strategic slip was recovered. After all, it had provided a realistic motivation and very close to reality.

The two of them finished their drink, Tony paid the bill and left the bar.

'The second helmet is a 50, is that all right with you?' Dick asked just outside.

The other one went away and asked:

'Shall we put these rags on now?'

'No need. We'll change before we make the last walk.'

Tony put on his helmet and sat in the back seat of the M-Scooter, a magnetic levitation motorcycle.

The two left for their destination.

Chapter 25

Brandon's communicator continued to report no line. His legs were begging for a little rest.

The idea of walking away seemed absurd and meaningless to him, but since nothing seemed normal that morning, he decided to take Tony's advice.

'On foot you'll be less visible and undetectable by traffic sensors. If, as I think, the communicative blackout is not accidental, someone could also have visual control of the area,' explained his colleague.

It was only a few kilometres to the Hidden City exit. He's been marching for hours now. The sunlight had gradually faded, gradually leaving room for the darkness that, colouring the sky black, had slowly enveloped the buildings piled up in that part of the city. The inhabitants of Old Town, and therefore also those of Hidden City, paradoxically could enjoy something that the wealthiest brothers of New Town, who were wrapped in the cage that blocked the ultraviolet rays, could only observe in scientific documentaries, or during excursions in the old part of the city: the sun and the moon. In New Town, in fact, the existence of the two stars was simulated by the computers of the meteorological service, which cleverly moved the ranks of a fictitious climate.

Tony stopped to catch his breath. He could already see the glitter of Old Town. Fragments of distant noises floated in the dilated air of the night. As soon as he was able to communicate, he would first call Thomas and then the editorial staff to ask someone to pick him up.

In the area where he was, he could see the moon. The real one.

The beep of the communicator caught his attention: the display had lit red. Now the signal was present. Brandon activated the communicator and selected Thomas' number. A dazzling light blocked it.

An M-Scooter's beacon was pointing at him. His eyesight went blank for a moment, while his pupils tried to adapt to the excessive brightness.

He turned his head to protect his eyes and escape that forced blindness. On the other side, another M-Scooter was gaining on him.

It took him a moment to understand. The two didn't seem to have peaceful intentions. At a glance, Brandon noticed that the M-Scooters were larger than an alleyway ten metres ahead.

The adrenaline gave his legs a new lease of life. With one click he leapt forward. From the diving suit worn by one of the two centaurs, a red light immediately turned into a laser beam that went off on the road, leaving a precise and deep groove.

Brandon jumped into the alley. He fell, but immediately got up and started running faster than his already debilitated physique allowed him.

After a few hundred metres he stopped and turned to look. The lights were gone. The two M-Scooters seemed to have disappeared into thin air. The young man took a big breath.

Just a few moments and a knot tightened around his throat. A light was pointing at him from above. The two guys were over his head now. They hadn't given up on their intentions and with the headlights off they had positioned themselves above the block.

Brandon flattened himself against the wall behind him, making it more difficult for his attackers to aim. He studied the situation and the area. The two M-Scooters had stood still. There were two reasons for this: they were waiting for orders from someone or waiting for the right time and position to strike. The ominous red light was still on.

He looked down to regain concentration and lucidity. The backlighting of the communicator caught his attention again. He forgot.

He had to warn Thomas at all costs, but he couldn't do it there. He could have been hit any second. He was too exposed.

It only took him a few moments to work out his plan. He would have suddenly snapped to the intersection in front of him and then turned left. This manoeuvre would have given him at least a ten-second lead, the next block was very high and would have forced the two centaurs to rise about thirty metres and then turn around the building.

Ten seconds would have been enough to send a voice message. Brandon activated the communicator. It was time. In his mind the countdown began: three, two, one.

He jumped forward and took the narrow road on the left as planned. In the race he began to record the message.

'We were discovered in Hidden City... Tony's in danger... He's meeting the tramp tonight... We split up, someone's shielded the area, they're after me. Help us! I'm in...'

A deaf cry interrupted those words.

This time the red light had caught him in the back, piercing him and passing him. If a large M-Scooter couldn't get through that alley, a laser beam certainly could.

Brandon fell to the floor. The pain in his back was blocking his breath. The cold of the earth quickly climbed up on him. He wanted to keep recording the message, but he couldn't move his lips or legs.

With the strength of his arms alone, he moved a few centimetres so that he could grab the fallen communicator a little further ahead. He placed his fingers on the SEND sign, the display swallowed the message and began processing. Another blade of light hit him. The communicator blew up along with the hand.

In his long career as a reporter, Brandon had also been involved in esotericism and he had a lot of information on life after death, on the supreme mystery of the passing. He had read in several texts that, before breathing his last breath, it was possible to see his life as in a film. In front of Brandon's eyes only a few episodes, the most significant ones: the moment of his graduation, the award ceremony of the Lewton-Stantford report, his wedding day, the birth of his daughter.

The pains all over his body attacked and swept those images. From above, the headlights kept flashing. He knew that that would be the last light he saw.

It happened.

The air was broken by the silence of his breath.

CHAPTER 26

Trevor and Tony had already worn the battered old clothes they'd brought along. They were on foot on their way to the meeting place. It was located on the west side of what had been the industrial area of the old town centuries before the New Day.

They walked at a fast pace, with Trevor in front, stopping occasionally to check his communicator. Every time he took a break, Tony would pick up the metre and a half that separated him from his colleague.

The landscape was uniform and monochromatic: an alternation of grey roads and large sheds of the same colour for several kilometres. Every corner looked the same as the adjacent one, the rusty signage was still essential to move around in there. A violent odour of dampness strained the nostrils. Some areas were illuminated by timid glow, others were shrouded in thick, impenetrable darkness.

Trevor broke the silence.

'If my information is correct, we should be very close.'

The two of them stopped for a moment. Trevor consulted the map on the communicator. Tony took a look at his, the display indicated the surprising presence of a signal. He didn't want to miss the opportunity and immediately activated the call to Thomas.

Trevor seemed to notice the gesture, but he didn't say anything.

Tony's communicator began processing. After a few moments a message dashed his hopes.

MISSING SIGNAL

The display, however, continued to indicate this.

Tony tried to play it cool. He was actually starting to understand. There were two hypotheses that could explain what had just happened, and both led to one person. His suspicions were becoming frightfully real. He decided, however, to wait. At that point, he just had to go through with it.

'Yes. I remembered. We're on the right side. A few more steps and we'll be there. Shall we go?'

Trevor blacked out the communicator.

'Let's go,' replied Tony, putting his in his pocket. In doing so, he noticed that the signal detector had turned off. His theory found a new confirmation.

They walked along a long gully and then turned left. In front of them stood a structure that had previously served as a hangar. From the inside came sounds that were unclear because they were muffled by the walls. An indistinct voice, of many people.

They'll go a few more metres. Trevor stopped, Tony did the same.

Between them and the entrance was a deserted road. They crossed it and covered the last few metres, keeping close to the wall.

'I hope your man is in there,' said Trevor with the conviction of a novice actor.

Tony didn't respond.

'The door is open. What are we going to do? Shall we go inside or see what's going on around?' the reporter asked.

'Follow me!' replied Trevor decisively.

He moved the door with his hand and they went in.

They didn't find what Tony expected. In fact, they found nothing. The big shed was completely empty. The sounds of that fictitious buzz continued to spread from above thanks to a player. A gloomy thread of light barely reflected on the large dark walls.

Trevor advanced.

Tony held his breath and this time he didn't follow him. He seized the opportunity to move away from his colleague and thus obtain space around him. His self-defence instructor had taught him: 'in a dangerous situation create space around you. You'll expand your defence solutions and gain valuable moments for any movement'.

Trevor picked up the communicator. He stared at him and waited.

Tony stayed in his place. He'd already realized that whatever happened from then on, he'd suffer it. He decided to play along to reserve any reaction at the appropriate time. He could have leveraged the surprise effect just once, and he didn't want to waste his chance.

After a couple of seconds he noticed that the colour of the display had changed.

He didn't have time to guess the reason why, from above, like streamers, about thirty men descended. It took a moment for them to plant themselves on the ground and surround them. Meanwhile, the descent cables had lost their soul and had collapsed to the ground.

Dick Trevor, without getting upset, passed his hand on the communicator to turn it off. He put it in the pocket sewn on his right leg. He seemed completely indifferent to what was going on around him.

He raised his head and looked up at Tony.

CHAPTER 27

Soccer Town was on the outskirts north of Hire City. The last Block to be built, it was a tribute to football fever, which remained the spasmodic one of the twentieth and twenty-first century, but now super structured in a more complex media-industrial structure than in the past. Stadiums, sports clubs, television stations, newspapers, residential centres for football players, were all concentrated in a single box, to offer citizens what the media called the "most beautiful show on the planet" and the most controversial "the most profitable show on the planet". To welcome his guests there was a huge football ball that reigned from above, suspended above the entrance gates. On the black and white pentagons ran the live images of the ninety-five thematic channels dedicated to the most popular sport in the state. In the dark of the evening, the alternating colours of the mega screens almost single-handedly illuminated the entrance area.

As he drove past it in his car, Daniel couldn't help but witness the broadcast of a furious fight, with kicks and punches, between two commentators. The most plausible cause was the difference of opinion as to whether a game action or a goal was regular or not. A lot of people were sure those fights were fake. Others, on the other hand, believed in the blood temperament of the interlocutors. Real or not, it looked like the beating was for real.

In the meantime, the on board computer exchanged data with that of the parking area operations centre, which imparted spatial coordinates to the Criton sensors in order to direct the vehicle to the free parking areas.

The image that stood out in front of him was that of a block organized in a morbidly symmetrical way. The left side was occupied by a chessboard of buildings used for the production activities of the football industry. On the right side earned the scene, instead, the famous fibre optic stadiums, ostentatious pride of Matt Bolsh. A little further on a gigantic village, equipped with every service and infrastructure, was reserved for the luxurious stay of the players.

The immense area between the east and west of the Block was invaded by hundreds of magnetic tubes for the mobility of people. A tangle of snakes wound through the central space and then crept into the two sides of Soccer Town and meandered through the folds of the different buildings. The interweaving followed a star-shaped structure, proceeded from a central node and then branched off towards the different destinations.

An acoustic signal brought Daniel's attention back to the on board monitor. The autopilot had just completed parking operations.

The precise movement of the hand made the message menu appear. He opened the one where Thomas gave him the address to meet. A simple command transferred the text to his communicator.

He got off the Criton and was guided by the moving carpet that led to the common entrance to all the tunnels. Waiting for him was the TS that the efficient parking management had sent him.

TS stood for Transport Sphere, small spherical individual mobility modules, the template that best suited the use in magnetic tunnels.

The TS sensor recorded his presence. The side opening closes and the control monitor requests the destination. Daniel called Thomas' message on his communicator and then typed: 19.95.4.277.

TS began to exhibit the usual tightrope walking variations. Inside, however, the traveller remained motionless thanks to sophisticated stabilization devices.

The eyes were on the control monitor, which provided the position, destination and time needed to reach it in real time: after seventy seconds, the Transport Sphere voice synthesizer decreed the end of the journey.

The structure of the building was circular. The outer belt was dedicated to the transit and disengagement between the studies placed in the inner part, divided into as many segments. When he reached the floor where Thomas was waiting for him, he turned left.

A swarm of people punctuated the two directions. The progress was frantic but composed, typical of those who work with the chronometer but know what to do and how to move. The entire level was dedicated to the direction and editing of the players' clinical data, as well as the production of all related talk shows.

Calcium *phagocytes* could subscribe to the clinical values of their favourites. They were able, that is, to display on their devices the physical condition of their favourite players, follow their state of health and endurance during the match, but also to evaluate their recovery in the days between the different league days. The subscription also included reports on surgical operations that the athlete might run into in the event of injury, including pre-operative visits, interviews with surgeons, paramedics and the lucky fan who, drawn from all subscribers, had won the chance to access the clinic to see for himself the condition of his idol.

The real-time collection and transmission of clinical data was ensured by a biochip installed subcutaneously in the chest area of the football player.

All this, in addition to meeting the spasmodic information needs of the "globists", allowed the organizational machine to reduce routine medical examinations to a simple data transfer. Considering the frequency of the commitments, the rhythm at which the players trained and the duration of cups and championships, now regularly distributed throughout the year and without intervals of more than two weeks, injuries were the order of the day and in certain seasons were the only breaks available to the athletes. Ligaments and menisci were monitored with painstaking care but this did not prevent players from injuring themselves with a certain regularity, forcing them to leave the competitive career shortly after the age of thirty.

Daniel walked past studio number twelve, where a conclave of surgeons discoursed about the successful outcome of the right crusader surgery of Clark Soprano, the centre forward of Nantos. The animated and composed discussion was broadcast on the screen outside the studio, for the use and consumption of visiting school groups.

A few metres before arriving at his destination, Daniel caught a glimpse of Thomas' face peeping out of studio one.

'I was looking forward to your arrival,' said the journalist, welcoming him with a smile. 'My doubts were well-founded. Come on.'

Waiting for them behind the control room panels was Maurice Billom. Daniel had never met him in person, but had seen him a few years earlier on television. He had been awarded at the TV Oscars for the editing of a documentary about the cultural degradation into which Hire City had plunged.

Forty-seven years old, well put physically, tanned, thick brown hair, pronounced cheekbone, watchful and expressive look. At that moment, he was sipping something from a glass.

Thomas made the necessary introductions.

'Maurice, this is Daniel.'

Daniel responded with a nod.

Maurice Billom came over and shook his hand.

'Make yourself comfortable,' he said. 'There's some big news to tell you. We have discovered...'

'Maurice discovered them more than anything else,' Thomas wanted to point out, 'in the videos I told you about before we separated at Central Hospital. By the way, were you able to talk to Josie?'

'Yes. The hair report is informal, but authentic. Unfortunately, so is the second. Katrine Johnson printed them both. Josie will verify the reliability of the organic find and try to trace it back to that unreadable substance.'

'All right,' replied Thomas. 'As for us, I am increasingly certain that Jerry is in danger. Correction: Jerry is definitely in danger.'

Daniel turned his eyes to Billom, who he added of his own,

'I don't know your friend, except for his football career. And I don't know if he's in danger now or not, but I can assure you that one of the videos is fake.'

Sipping from the glass he held between his fingers, he approached the control area. He put it on the table and retrieved a burger left halfway through just before Daniel came in.

'It's a very good fake, the work of excellent professionals,' repeated Thomas.

'What's the footage?' Daniel asked.

'Just give me two seconds and I'll explain everything,' replied Billom. Thomas also wanted to give a few more explanations.

'I happened to see an interview with Jerry on Soccer News a few days ago. It is notorious that most of the time these interviews are prepared at the desk and have only a propaganda purpose, but something upset me and I could not understand what. Then I realized. Maurice, you may start.'

The precise and coordinated movements of Billom's hands on the console activated the big screen on the left. It was playing the sequences of a football match. Moments later the screen on the right also came to life and proposed Jerry's interview at Soccer Eden.

Seeing Jerry again after such a long time caused his heart to shake, no matter how well disguised. The last time he had seen him was, again on television, during a sports show that he had accidentally seen while zapping.

He continued to hate him because of that betrayal, and because of the consequences he had had on his psyche: he had never been able to trust anyone, nor to become as attached as he once was.

Judging by the pictures, Jerry didn't look too old. He answered his interviewer's questions while in a swimsuit on a beautiful artificial beach. From time to time, the recreational facilities of Soccer Eden appeared as an interlude.

'I'm ready,' said Billom.

'Go ahead,' encouraged Thomas.

'Here on the left are pictures of Niosen-Karlemstone, one of the last games Jerry played. He's number thirteen. Here are some frames from the game. They're the ones we're interested in.'

The commands given to the console made the images of the game in the top left corner smaller. Billom added:

'On the right is a very recent interview with Jerry. According to the overlay headlines, the recording would have been made on the 15th of last month.'

Meanwhile, the two screens had merged into one and the images transmitted by Football Eden appeared enlarged.

'Doesn't that ring a bell?' Thomas asked, looking like he already knew the answer.

Daniel plucked his eyebrows and for the first time opened his mouth.

'No,' he answered honestly.

The images of some games interspersed with Jerry's under the clutches of the interviewer. As soon as the shot returned to the football player, Thomas pressed him.

'How can you not see anything?'

Daniel didn't focus. Thomas then decided to unblock the stalemate of the friend with a conclusive clue.

'Look at his hands.'

Quiet.

It took a moment to focus.

Daniel understood.

CHAPTER 28

'Who did he meet at Central Hospital?'
'Dr Josie Smith.'
'Is he still there?'
'No, Captain. He's in the Soccer Town TV studios.'
'What did he go there to do?'
'We don't know yet.'
'Find out.'
'It will be done. We don't let him out of our sight.'

Chapter 29

The fingers of Jerry's right hand were repeatedly asking for help, using precisely the code invented by Daniel at the time of Father George's oratory.

Daniel's expression was more than eloquent. He understood. Thomas seized the moment.

'Yes, they are your "talking fingers".'

The message was clear. He never forgot that code. Retracted index and middle finger with protruding finger ring and pinkie were for the letter H. Index and middle finger slightly overlapped with the ring and pinkie finger withdrawn indicated E. The ring finger touching the palm indicated the L. The thumb resting on the middle finger aligned with the other three fingers identified P.

Not knowing when his hands would return to the frame, Jerry kept repeating the message throughout the interview.

'There's more, Daniel,' continued Thomas. 'The footage is manipulated.'

'They want to make it look like it was only shot a few days ago. Instead it refers to four years ago, basically at the time of Jerry's last games,' Billom continued. 'I'll show you right now. Watch it.'

Now it was the turn of his technological devilry.

'On the left we have an image of Jerry's face taken from the game four years ago. On the right is an extrapolation from the interview. Notice anything?'

'He looks slightly older,' commented Daniel.

'Exactly! Day after day we don't notice it, but four years later something on our face inevitably changes. We don't realize it until we see our pictures from a few years back.

That's exactly why you noticed a slight aging on Jerry's face.'

Daniel listened while waiting to see where he was going with it.

'Now I'm manipulating Jerry's image with AgePro. In cases like this, it is the best simulation software on the market. Given the high cost, only we in Soccer Town and the police use it.'

Thomas went back into the speech to give his friend a few more explanations.

'Here in Soccer Town, the editors of those stupid gossip shows use it. Often and willingly even the most famous hosts get some touch-ups on video. Of course, the police use it for identikit. Sorry to interrupt, Maurice. Go ahead.'

Billom's hands went back to work on the console.

'Let's age the features of Jerry taken from the game video to bring him back to the present day.'

The image of the face, four years earlier, was now crossed by a continuous line running from top to bottom across the entire width of the screen. The result was an image identical to the one extracted from the interview.

'As you can see, they're the same. The state of aging of the face is identical, and not only at a glance,' Thomas intervened.

'That's right,' confirmed Billom. 'If we subit the two images to computer comparison, we have confirmation that they are perfectly superimposable, wrinkle by wrinkle, capillary by capillary. This comparison software also detects the state of elasticity of the tissues.'

Meanwhile, the monitor had preceded its user, processing the message: MATCH 100%.

Daniel remained silent. Maurice and Thomas' arguments only showed that the two images differed by four years, as did the dates on the overlay. He was aware that the two would lead him to the final conclusions, but he did not understand the keystone of the discourse.

Thomas got to the point.

'As sophisticated and technologically advanced as AgePro is, its simulations cannot be perfect. The aging process depends on too many psychic, physical and environmental variables, and cannot be entirely predictable by any software that exists on the face of the earth.'

'If we took an image of you from four years ago and ground it under AgePro,' Billom assumed, 'it would produce a remarkably realistic image of your current state of aging, but not quite the same.'

Daniel was beginning to understand.

'The differences between the simulation and the real state wouldn't be visible to the naked eye, but a standard graphic comparison software would show them,' Billom continued.

'And in Jerry's case, the overlap was perfect,' remarked Daniel, demonstrating that he understood the meaning of the discourse. In the meantime, the big screen had been cleaned and now housed two images of Billom's face.

'The one on the left is a picture of me from a few years ago. On the right, one taken yesterday. For me too, as you can see, the years jump a little bit. Now I set the AgePro… and here is my simulated image today: the photos look identical, but look what the comparison software tells us.'

On the monitor, the writing had changed.

MATCH 97%. DIFFERENCES DETECTED: 547

'Let's visualize a difference at random.'

A dot at cheekbone height widened to reveal a very small wrinkle. On the simulated image it appeared deeper and slightly longer.

'Have you used more anti-aging creams than your software could have predicted?' Daniel asked in the tone of those who understood.

'I've never used creams in my life. Much more simply, as already mentioned, there are too many and above all unpredictable circumstances that determine our ageing process.'

'You've convinced yourself now that Jerry's in danger?' Thomas pushed him. 'Do you think it makes sense to fake a four-year-old interview with AgePro if you've got football players loafing around all day and they're fully available there at Soccer Eden? And anyway, in that video, Jerry's asking us for help.'

Daniel nodded.

'Guys, I'm done,' Billom concluded. 'If you need anything else, say it now, because I've got McLace's meniscus surgery to monitor later on.'

'That's all right, Maurice, I don't want to abuse your courtesy. You've been a great help. I hope one day I can return the favour.'

'Wait a minute,' Daniel said. 'I'd like some more information about Robert Konnor, if you don't mind.'

'I've already talked to Thomas about it, after all I know as much as he does,' explained Maurice. 'Awesome skills, money to spare, a beautiful wife, the usual trifling gossip and rituals.'

'Can you tell me anything about his background?'

'He's been a phenomenon since he was a little boy. He was the son of one of Soccer Town's leading medical engineers, Vincent Konnor.'

'Can you make an appointment with him? After all, it is his father. He could provide us with valuable information about his son, as well as Katrine Johnson.'

'Impossible, he died a few months ago. The official Soccer Town statement spoke of a heart attack, although it has to be said that they are very buttoned up at the medical centre and have few relations with the outside world. I think he may have been involved in some accident in Area 51. At least that's what the wicked tongues say, who, I must say, often get it right.'

'What's Area 51?' Daniel asked.

'That's the nickname we Soccer Town workers give the medical research department, for the halo of secrecy and mystery that surrounds it. Like the famous Area 51 of the 20th century, you know?'

'So you think Vincent Konnor was a victim of some dangerous experiment?'

'I don't know. Surely, no one believes in a heart attack. One of Soccer Town's top scientists dying of a heart attack in the temple of medical engineering!'

Daniel shrugged. He didn't know what to say. Thomas changed the subject.

'Any important events in the last few months of Robert Konnor's career? Can you tell us anything else?'

'A multimillion-dollar contract with McStyling to advertise a hair gel: ChangeHead.'

'Yes, I know it,' Thomas said. 'Even my son uses it when he goes to parties. It's a gel that makes your hair change colour, at will.'

'That's right. There were fierce legal battles from HairSystem, with which Robert Konnor had a previous contract and which he terminated after McStyling's pharaonic offer. Konnor's turn-around caused the HairSystem a considerable loss of money.'

'Surely they didn't take it well!' commented Thomas. 'You were invaluable Maurice. We have to go now.'

'One more moment,' begged Daniel. He put his hands in his pocket and showed the card he had taken from Johnson. 'Can you tell me what this is? Whether it's an obsolete card,

I got there on my own, but I didn't go any further.'

Maurice Billom's eyes lit up.

'Obsolete will be the three of us, Daniel! You're holding in your hand one of the latest technological advances from bioengineering. It is a DNA key and its rightful owner, who given the question should not be you, must have something valuable held at Union Bank.'

'The Union Bank, of course. I had guessed it, but I couldn't understand how it could be connected to such an ancient model card. At least that's what it looked like. I teach history and I don't know about that stuff. What's a DNA key?'

'A state-of-the-art security key. The oval grooves you see on both sides are the thumb and index finger housing. It detects the DNA of the person holding it, you know. Within a few millimetres of thickness there are years of studies and the best molecular nanotechnology. This system allows you to be sure that the key is literally in the hands of its rightful owner. I know Union Bank uses them for their safety deposit boxes, but I have to admit that, in fact, an untrained eye can mistake this little toy for an old microchip card. The designer who designed it probably married a retro taste that has been going great for a few years.'

Maurice Billom was proving to be a real expert on the subject. Daniel decided to take the opportunity to remove another doubt.

'One last thing, Maurice. It's fair to say that each individual's iris is unique, right?'

'Of course! But I think I can be of more help to you if you also explain the reason for the question. Yours is not a simple scientific curiosity, I think.'

'You're right. I'll rephrase the question: if an eye-escanner-controlled security system allows me access, does that mean that my iris map is included in its database?'

'Could be. But it's more likely he only knows your DNA from Shefner's area. It is a faster and less complicated method than scanning the entire iris. By now all the latest eye scanners only analyse that section.'

Daniel thought a bioengineering expert like him was wasted on the job. He remained silent to hear his explanation.

'Until twenty years ago it was thought that the map of the iris striations and DNA were not related to each other, proof was that twins also possessed different irises. Shefner discovered that a particular section of the iris is directly related to the sequence of adenine, guanine, cytosine and thymine present in a specific part of our genetic code. You only need to know your DNA to check whether or not the iris read by a security system's eye scanner is yours or not, making it unnecessary to scan the entire surface. I bet the light emitted by the eye scanner was purple,' he finally ventured.

Billom was right. In his local mind, Daniel remembered that the purple light also connected him to another enigmatic situation: the access to the bunker at Villa Konnor. However, he preferred not to mention it at all.

'Yes, you're right,' he replied.

'Then it was a Shefner-based eye scanner. After all, the wavelength of purple is the most suitable when it comes to DNA. Your Union Bank card uses that too.'

'Thank you, Maurice, you've been a tremendous help. At this point, all I have to do is one last thing: A trip to Union Bank...'

CHAPTER 30

Tony felt a knot in his throat. He was no stranger to dangerous situations, working with Thomas Lewton meant being in the trenches all the time, but this time it was different. He felt overwhelmed by events.

Dick Trevor was staring at him. He came a few steps closer, stopping a couple of spurs away from him. The gunmen stood still.

'Tony Stantford, Thomas Lewton's right-hand man. Right?' he asked out of the blue. Tony decided not to answer. He wondered how long his cover had been blown, but at that point the answer was irrelevant. 'I'm the "weird guy" you've been looking for, Tony. Believe it or not, I just saved your life,' Trevor continued. 'Just don't call me SJ023H. Jerry it is fine. Jerry Crenna.'

Jerry Crenna. That name wasn't new to him, but he couldn't remember why. His eyes stared and lost in the void revealed his bewilderment.

'I realize I haven't been much of a character, but I think Thomas Lewton told you about me. If I show you some dribbling...'

Tony understood and for further confirmation he stared at the faces of the other men. They were all former football players. Jerry showed a sincere smile and put out his right hand.

'Welcome, Mr Stantford. It took time to pick up the signal. Some of us almost didn't believe it anymore,' continued Jerry, who held his hand in mid-air. Tony held it with understandable uncertainty. 'I couldn't tell you right away who I really was because we're all monitored and spied on out there. We'd have taken too many risks, you and me both, and my cover as Dick Trevor would have been blown.'

Jerry's tone was more relaxed now.

'I think you owe me an explanation, Dick...or rather, Jerry,' Tony replied. 'First, I'd like to know how you know Thomas Lewton.'

'He's my...friend.'

A moment of hesitation broke the sentence, as if that word had stuck in his throat. Jerry felt the need to clarify.

'I don't know if I should say *he was* a friend of mine. But that's another story. In any case I think that friendship between two people either exists or does not exist, it cannot disappear and reappear. The fact that you're here proves it.'

Tony didn't feel like saying he'd infiltrated Hidden City just for a journalistic inquiry. At least for the time being. Jerry took the communicator out of his pocket and looked at it.

'We're still shielded by our guys, but we need to move. The green signal won't last long on this thing.'

Tony looked away to peek at the display of his communicator. Jerry noticed and anticipated his questions.

'Yeah, your communicator's not freaking out. It detects my transmission bandwidth, but obviously, it can't work. My signal uses an encrypted bridge, filters communications within the team.'

'By "the team" you mean them?' Tony asked, pointing to the men surrounding them.

Jerry nodded.

'We'd better move to our shelter. We need to stay undisturbed because I think you have a lot of questions.'

A man moved out of the group and approached the two of them.

'Jerry, we need to go. We only have 110 seconds of coverage left. The armouring of the signal could then arouse suspicion.'

'Yes, you're right. I've already thought about it. Give the go-ahead to the guys.'

A movement of the hand brought the other men closer. A jolt to the ground alarmed Tony.

'Don't worry, we're coming down to our secret hideaway. We'll be really safe there,' Jerry reassured him.

The central part of the hangar floor had turned out to be a self-propelled platform, and now it was leading them down. The void left by his disappearance was supplemented by a side-sliding hatch.

'When Thomas found out about a guy named SJ023H, he ordered me to find you and drop everything else. What does this acronym mean?' Tony asked.

'It doesn't mean anything and it means everything at the same time. It's a little stupid, 30-year-old teenage thing, but it worked. It was a secret code to use in case of danger. I hoped Thomas or someone else would remember, though I feared not.'

The group of men was already at minus 20 metres.

'Why are you hiding?' Tony asked again.

'It's an old story. I was thrown into this place a few years ago, but I've only been *reborn* for a year and a half. Since then, I've actively participated in the rebellion movement and managed to infiltrate the vigilantes.'

'Are you reborn? What does that mean?'

That term caught Tony's attention. Meanwhile, the platform had reached its destination. They were 40 metres below the ground. In front of them there was a large corridor with dark, irregular walls.

'Follow me! There's someone I want you to meet first. He's one of the last to arrive, but he's the most important. He gave our movement a breakthrough and is the only one who came here aware of what was happening around him. He, surely, will need no introduction.'

Jerry was moving at a fast pace and Tony was trying to stay by his side. In the meantime, the other men had vanished through the numerous crossroads that ran around every corner.

'We have to thank some wealthy 21st century crooks if we can use this place now. I think it was a narcotics storage facility, used by the underworld before the big exodus that led to New Day. It came in handy. We're pretty safe down here, but we still have to be careful. Our enemies are well organized and above all unscrupulous. We've only made it this far because they still think we're empty and aren't afraid of us.'

Tony would have wanted to ask more questions, but he realized it wasn't the right time. No small quality for a reporter.

After a few metres the spaces were reduced. The gully they were walking along tightened like a funnel and flowed into a large room without doors, signalled only by an arch.

There was a man in there with his back to the entrance. The room was bare, in the middle a large table and several maps on top of each other. There were a dozen or so chairs in poor condition around it. In the upper part of the walls, some grates guaranteed the supply of air to the environment. They were definitely connected to level zero.

'Your SJ023H brought home the result, champ!'

The bent man on the maps raised his head and while remaining with his hands resting on the table he turned around.

Tony recognized him immediately and, after keeping his mouth shut until then, he spoke for the first time.

'What kind of trouble are you guys in? Now you're going to stop a while and explain everything. From the beginning,' he ordered with the authority of those who, after a bad quarter of an hour, have the right to claim clarification.

Jerry smiled.

'I told you he wouldn't need an introduction. Sit down! It's time to figure things out.'

CHAPTER 31

The Transport Sphere had just begun its silent run.
Left Criton in the parking lot of Block 37, Thomas and Daniel were on their way to Union Bank headquarters.
Daniel held the card given to him by Katrine Johnson and turned it nervously from side to side, over and over again. He'd been thinking about that thing all night. After leaving Maurice Billom's study, he had taken Thomas to the News Building and rushed straight home to be pampered by Miss Carson's delicacies.
After dinner he retired to his room trying to fall asleep right away. He couldn't do it. The thought of what he might discover the next day in that safe deposit box had not left him until the first glow of dawn, when he was taken hostage by Morpheus for a few hours.
Finally, the weather service in Hire City had finally made the sun rise that morning too. And now, perhaps, he was closer to the answers he was looking for.
'How did it go with Josie?' Thomas asked.
'The report on the hair is...'
'You know what I mean!'
Denying the importance of that meeting would have meant a barrage of additional questions. He then decided to admit the truth.
'It was good to see her again, if that's what you wanted to hear,' replied Daniel nervously stroking his beard.
'I had already figured it out for myself. I was referring to...something more than just pleasure, that's all.'
It was to be expected that he understood everything; they knew each other too well and for too long. Willingly or not,

for once he had to take off his armour and ask his friend for the honour of arms.

In fact, the meeting at Central Hospital had brought to light Daniel's real feelings for Josie, taking him by surprise too, now certain that he had relegated them to a distant past. He was staggered and frightened that Josie's return might undermine the rationality with which he tended to protect himself and reject people, the world, and relationships that were too demanding.

Prey to doubt, he decided to open up. Surely, he could trust Thomas.

'It was more than pleasant to see her again,' he admitted, arching his eyebrows and finally showing off an accomplice's smile. He'd shaken off a lot of weight. 'But I don't know exactly how I feel either, so don't travel too far with the fantasy.'

'I think you understand what this is all about. You're just afraid to admit it.'

The hiss of a communicator interrupted the conversation. That was Josie. Daniel took a deep breath and answered. The image of the friend appeared on the display.

'Hello, Daniel. I have news for you.'

'Good to see you, Josie. Good or bad?'

'If they're good or bad, I don't know, but I need you to send me your fingerprints immediately. Oh! I see you're with Thomas. Bye.'

Thomas replied with a nod of his hand.

'What do you need them for?' Daniel asked.

'The usual mistrusting. Just send them.'

Josie's tone was very confidential.

'Okay. How about my thumb?'

'I'm fine with anything about you, even your thumb.'

Daniel placed his finger on the display of the communicator, which immediately acquired the fingerprint and sent it to Josie.

'What's this about?'

'Just give me a few seconds and I'll tell you everything. I need to check something I think I already know.'

Thomas watched the scene compassed, without comment. Within himself, however, he rejoiced at the newfound feeling between his friends, and held back a sly smile.

'Here we go, guys. That's what I thought. Listen to this.'

Daniel and Thomas had their ears up.

'I have recovered the artefacts on which Johnson conducted her private analysis. It's a comb and a hair.'

'The reports I found at the mansion are authentic, so what?' Daniel interrupted her.

'Yes, and not only that. The most important thing is that the results are also accurate. That hair really does have your DNA. As the head of the genetics centre, I have access to the FDDB and took the liberty of verifying it.'

'That hair has Daniel's DNA, but you didn't say it was his. Right?' Thomas asked.

'You hit the nail on the head. I ran the prints on the comb and got two donors. One is Dr Johnson, whose fingerprints we have as an employee of this facility. The other, presumably the owner of the hair, is not present in our databases nor in the federal ones. At this point, I also analysed the prints on the report. I found five donors. The first one is you, Daniel, and I confirmed it a moment ago by checking the print you sent me. The other three prints are mine, Thomas and Johnson's. I pulled Thomas' prints off the press database. Guess who's the fifth donor?'

'The owner of the comb, I suppose,' Daniel intervened.

'Exactly! As for the second report, we know the foetus in Johnson's lap had the same DNA as you, so there are two cases. The hair and baby are yours, or hair and baby are another man's, I would say Robert Konnor, and you both have the same DNA. Being different people, you obviously have different fingerprints.'

'A twin thirty years younger? I don't think so,' commented Thomas. 'Josie, are you sure Robert Konnor has the same DNA as Daniel?'

'Strictly speaking, no, because I'm not sure that that hair is not Daniel's. After all, we ignore both Robert Konnor's DNA and fingerprints, so mine is not a thesis, just a hypothesis. Although I don't think Daniel at his venerable age uses elettrociclogel.'

'What are you talking about, Josie?'

Daniel overlooked the term "venerable". He was going to hold it against her later.

'It is the mysterious substance on the hair. We're talking about a synthetic molecule produced by McStyling.'

'A gel that changes hair colour?'

'That's right. How do you know?'

'It was advertised by Robert Konnor, Maurice Billom told us. Strange coincidence, don't you think?'

'I never believed in more than two coincidences put one after the other,' commented Thomas.

Josie resumed her considerations.

'The natural thing to do seemed to me to check Konnor's DNA on file for a possible match.'

'I was going to ask you, though I had no doubt you'd already thought of it yourself. Why, then, do you still have these doubts about genetic matching?'

'There is no Robert Konnor. According to the gene bank, Johnson's husband doesn't exist or never did.'

'It is quite unlikely that a "non-existent" guy could have become one of the most famous sportsmen of the last three hundred years,' Thomas objected. 'There's no way they didn't notice anything in Soccer Town.'

Josie nodded.

'Something's wrong with me too, and I think some answers can be found at the Soccer Town medical centre. I'm going right over there to check it out.'

'Are you talking about Area 51?'

'That one. I see you know its nickname too,' Josie marvelled. 'I have an appointment with Dr Vivian this morning. She's a friend who owes me a lot of favours and it's time to cash them in. I'll also take this opportunity to ask a few questions about Jerry. I haven't forgotten the other emergency at all.'

'Trouble, unfortunately, never comes alone,' commented Thomas.

'Be careful. The longer this goes on, the more I don't like it. I wouldn't want to take any unnecessary risks,' Daniel recommended to her with great care.

'Don't worry, I can take care of myself. You guys keep me posted on Jerry. I don't think there's any news about him, or you'd have told me about it.'

'Well, actually, there is something, but it's not very good...'

Thomas summarized the latest events, heard with growing concern by Josie.

'Let's just hope we can find him as soon as possible,' he said in his haste to end the conversation. 'Fingers crossed. I'll run to Area 51, hope I don't run into any angry aliens. Let's keep up to date.'

'You can count on it,' replied the other two almost in chorus.

Josie greeted with a wave of her hand, just before her image disappeared from the display.

'Do you think Josie over there can find any answers?'

Daniel asked Thomas.

'I certainly hope so.'

Transport Sphere's edgy voice got in the way of their speeches.

'Destination reached. Union Bank. Headquarters. Level Zero.'

The sphere hatch from the left side.

Chapter 32

'Captain, we have concluded the first part of our intervention.'

'Have you encountered any problems, Trenton?'

'No one, sir. They didn't put up any resistance.'

'Any word from the targets?'

'We're still cross-referencing our information with neutralized subjects.'

'Any results?'

'Yes, sir. We don't know exactly where they are yet, but they certainly exist and are here somewhere. It's only a matter of hours. The team is ready.'

'Well done, Trenton. I had no doubt.'

'Only one problem, Captain.'

'Which one?'

'A code black we couldn't avoid in time.'

'Who is it? One of them?'

'I don't think so. Lieutenant Charit is handling it.'

'As of this moment, it will be dark communicative for at least twenty-four hours. I'm on my way to Area 51 and it's too dangerous there.'

'I understand, sir.'

'That's all for now. Good luck, Trenton.'

'Thank you, sir.'

'Over and out.'

Chapter 33

The building that housed the Union Bank headquarters was the tallest in Block 37. The credit institute's fiery red sign stood five hundred metres high in a parallelepiped entirely in gold colour, punctuated by the openings of the more than two thousand offices that made it up and edged the envelope. The iridescent shades of the outer crystals redesigned its appearance from time to time, like a soubrette changing her dress during the show. The imposing hall had a hundred monitors on the walls, which attacked the client from all sides. Above, millions of levitating lights dotted the ceiling and radiated light into the huge entrance hall.

Anyone who entered that place would have felt like a tiny dot lost inside a huge white sheet of paper.

Two black dots had just stopped by the front desk. They were Daniel and Thomas.

'You don't need an ID at all, just your person and the DNA key in your hand. The cassette is encrypted and to the bearer,' clarified the employee in charge of sorting customer requests. A plaque placed in front of his station bore the name Marco Wonder.

'Yes. I'm aware of that. It was just an excess of zeal,' Daniel pointed out, so that he didn't realize he was going in there for the first time.

'I just need your card for a few seconds. This way, I can have it taken to the right vault,' continued the officer.

Daniel reached out his hand and handed it to him.

Mr Wonder grabbed the card and put it in a slot on the right side of the terminal.

He waited for a few moments. Daniel and Thomas did

the same.

'That's it! Mr Mistade will accompany you to vault number one hundred and two,' resumed the employee back, returning the card to its rightful owner and pointing to a person waiting behind them. 'The regulation only allows access to the vaults for one person,' he continued.

Daniel caught his friend's eye. They didn't say anything to each other. Then he turned around.

'Please follow me,' said Mistade in a formal tone.

They took the corridor that opened a few metres ahead, to the right of the reception. They reached the lift and once inside they waited. The entire route of the two men had already been centrally planned and was followed by the security department.

On the wall opposite the lift entrance a huge zero appeared. The latter, after a few moments, was replaced by the numerical indications of the plans that were going past. The numbers were negative. The elevator was going underground. It only took a few seconds for that rapid succession of numbers to stop at minus twenty-four. The doors open again.

Another corridor, CCTV cameras everywhere. Then a door. Mistade stopped and waited for the command centre to give consent. A few seconds later, the door opened and disappeared into the walls. The chaperone led the way.

The hundred and two vault consisted of a room higher than wide, the sidewalls were entirely occupied by about four thousand safes. The only furniture inside was a long, narrow table flanked by a console table.

Mr Mistade waited a few more seconds. A message appeared on the console monitor:

ACTIVE

Then he broke the silence.

'You may enter your DNA card, sir. Keep your thumb and forefinger firmly in the thumb and index finger in the thumb slot.'

Daniel followed the instructions with the utmost care, like a schoolboy. The message on the monitor had changed.

RECOGNIZED DNA. ENTER PASSWORD

'At this point I must leave you, sir. My job is to remind you that you only have three attempts available, should you make a mistake in entering your password. When you're done, take out the card. I'll be out here to escort you out,' said Mr Mistade impassively, who turned his back and walked away in silence.

Daniel waited for his escort to leave and the door to close.

Now he was alone. He and that monitor demanded an answer to your question. 'If I have the same DNA as that guy, then I have no other choice: I have to reason like him, that is I have to be him, that is myself,' he thought confusingly. 'What password would I give?' he kept asking himself, while trying to stay calm and lucid.

Daniel used to look for obvious hiding places or passwords. He was thinking the other way around. -In fact, he believed that the discounted passwords were discarded first by the bad guys, precisely because of their nature.

He typed ROBERT.

The yellow squares that replaced the letters faded until they disappeared completely.

The message on the monitor immediately disappointed him.

INCORRECT PASSWORD

Without even thinking, he quickly typed KATRINE.

The hand was faster than his self-control. Too late now: another attempt had been lost.

He took a deep breath in and bent his eyes on the table to

gather mental energy. He tried, once again, to imagine how he would behave if he were in Robert Konnor's place.

The answer was always, 'I would have put my name.'

Robert's name, however, was not liked by the access system, and neither was Katrine's.

A single word prevented him, perhaps, from getting any closer to the truth. By a bizarre association of ideas, he was reminded of Robert Konnor's last words, heard in the bunker of the villa: *'remember this name: Daniel...'.*

Maybe he was thinking right up to that point. He just had the wrong person. That was probably the password, and yet he didn't have the courage to type it in.

His rational side required him to think again. At the same time, he pointed out that any other argument would drag him into a field of immense possibilities, where he would have no chance of success. Might as well have played that last hunch.

The room seemed to get smaller. He decided to type that name slowly, to avoid mistakes. Letter after letter, the entry was confirmed by the sparkle of the small square that appeared for each character selected. The first had replaced the ominous error warning. Four more were added one after the other. The last one was missing.

He held his breath.

He brought his finger closer to the virtual keyboard of the console, at the letter "L".

The yellow squares disappeared on the monitor, but no writing appeared. Daniel didn't know how to interpret this. The lack of the error message could be assessed positively... or not?

The answer was not long in coming.

A gap opened up on the left side of the table. A metal box emerged from below. At the end of its run, it opened automatically, letting out a black cylinder. Daniel took it and opened it. Inside it held a mem-chip, a common external memory medium that could hold anything. The likely answers to his questions were postponed. He should have at least reached his Criton before he discovered the contents of that memory. He put the chip inside the case and put everything in his pocket.

On the monitor, meanwhile, was displayed the report of the last and only three accesses to the safe deposit box.

28 November 2255 - 10:13 a.m.
29 November 2255 - 09:29 a.m.
29 November 2255 - 10:13 a.m.

The date of the 29th November, the day of Robert Konnor's disappearance, came back forcefully. Perhaps the last thing the football player had done before he disappeared into thin air was to visit Union Bank.

At the bottom a message reminded him that to close the cassette he would have to take his card out of the slot after finishing.

He took one last look at the dates. It was enough to memorize them.

Pulled the card out, the metal box automatically closed.

The vault door, meanwhile, had also opened and Mr Mistade was waiting there with his back to the entrance. A moment later, without getting too unperturbed, he had already started to make his way again, this time in the opposite direction, the covered route a few minutes earlier.

Mistade's gait seemed frightfully slow to him. He couldn't wait to get out of that place to see the contents of the mem-chip. On more than one occasion, he almost pinched his feet from behind.

After fifteen interminable seconds, they arrived at the lift. The two of them went in and had to wait a few moments for that box of mirrors to start up on its own. Daniel stared at the wall in front of him to watch the countdown offered by the display. In his eyes, the numbers seemed to stumble together, as if they couldn't stumble at the right speed.

Finally the zero appeared.

The lift doors opened. Between him and the contents of the chip, there was only the last corridor, the entrance hall, the access route to the parking area and the Criton reader.

As we arrived at the lobby, the impeccable Mistade dismissed his guest.

'My work is done. It's been a pleasure serving you. I give my regards.'

'Thank you. Have a good day,' replied Daniel, then turned towards the exit. Thomas was waiting for him. The trajectories of their looks intersected and then overlapped.

Thomas tried to read in his friend's eyes. Daniel half-closed his eyelids to raise them up immediately afterwards and put his hand near his trouser pocket. The journalist friend understood. Daniel found something in that safe deposit box.

They both headed for the exit. Their footsteps reunited in the entrance square.

Thomas took the floor.

'It's in your pocket, isn't it?'

'Yes. It's a mem-chip. We just need to get to the Criton reader.'

They used the TS that connected the bank to the parking lots. After a few minutes, they were already on the treadmill that would lead them to the car.

They were not content to be transported, so they began to walk the carpet at a rapid pace, gaining precious seconds.

When they arrived at their destination, Daniel's M-Car opened up before the two got close. They went in. The Criton closed and went dark.

Daniel took the case out of his pocket and showed the chip to his friend, then inserted it into the reader.

The on board display switches on automatically. A man in a white coat, in his seventies, appeared, filmed in half-bust. The field of vision was fixed. Surely, it was a static shot, made by the same person who was pointing the lens.

Thomas had a tremor, shaking his head slightly upwards. Daniel noticed.

'Do you know him?' he asked.

'I think so,' replied the friend.

The man in the white coat started talking.

CHAPTER 34

'They just got out of Union Bank.'
'Did you set up the receiver?'
'Of course, there's no Criton that can resist me.'
'Fine.'
'I plugged the receiver directly into the vehicle's central system. From this moment on, it will be their shadow.'
'Yes, I can see that. I'm already getting the signal. They're watching a video. I have the main character and his white coat on my monitor. Job well done. Over and out.'
'Roger, Captain.'

CHAPTER 35

'Robert, I wish I never had to record this video. For several years now, I've feared this moment might come...'

The framed figure in the monitor froze and breathed deeply to regain calm and lucidity. Daniel took advantage of the break to point at his friend with an interrogative air. Thomas got the message and complied with the legitimate request.

'This is Dr Vincent Konnor...'

'Robert's father?'

'That's the one.'

The two remained silent again.

'If you're listening to me, that means I'm not with you anymore. I've instructed Union Bank to give you a DNA card if I didn't show up within 12 hours, to give you access to the safe deposit box where you found this mem-chip. It's too late for me now. You, on the other hand, can still make it. To help you in this dangerous situation, I'm forced to reveal information that I've kept hidden for a lifetime. It all started 29 years ago, when...'

Dr Konnor hesitated. It was visibly proven, in body and spirit. He narrowed his eyes and tightened his jaw, then regained the necessary self-control.

'...when I was forced to create you,' he revealed. 'Your mother and I aren't your real parents. I mean your biological parents, because in our hearts you have always been, and always will be, our son.'

Another emotional discharge created a void in Dr Konnor's throat. He resumed speaking with increasing discomfort.

'29 years ago, you were born out of a cloning machine to satisfy the ambitions and whims of Simon Malcolm, the father-master of Soccer Town. Basically a lunatic. At the time the world of football was in decline, talent was scarce and people were thinking about much more important things. There wasn't a single team that had a balance sheet in the black. Malcolm understood that in order to relaunch football, it was necessary to make it spectacular, to invest in athletes capable of offering a show within the show. "Panem et circenses" the Latins used to say. The fan became an integral part of the match, he could and should know every detail of his idols, subscribe to increasingly expensive and increasingly unnecessary services, as long as he was able to make him feel like the twelfth man on the field, a concept that clubs have always used to foment cheering and increase the number of subscribers. Football players who were more prepared or prone to lying immediately became stars, half gods who touched the ball and scored a goal, or prevented it with disarming ease. All bullshit. Hence the match-fixing, scandals and artfully created injuries. Weddings never celebrated with the starlet on duty, controversy born on Monday and forgotten on Tuesday, prizes awarded to unworthy football players just to make people talk in bars. Get Football Betting Investigations: it wasn't just the games that were rigged, it was the investigations as well! It wasn't really investigating anyone, it was all a farce. The important thing for Malcolm was people talking about Soccer Town and its phenomena. He'd been fed up with ordinary players for some time, no matter how capable. He was looking for the perfect player, the one who could attract the attention of every fan. Dr Vivian drew up a report full of medical parameters in order to scientifically establish the value of a football player and his potential. Physical, psychological and even environmental characteristics came together in a sort of vademecum that Malcolm followed literally in his search for his "man". He found him, or thought he did, in a young talent, but he couldn't hire him. He then decided to resort to cloning. The only alternative he had left to achieve *absolute certainty of billionaire earnings. He used it without remorse. Kidnapping him wouldn't have solved the situation, or he wouldn't have backed out. He's capable of far worse things. The point is, a sad football player wouldn't have worked out 100%. His henchmen tried until the end to sign him, enticing the family with dizzying figures. No way. He never made it to Soccer Town, fortunately for him. The boy's name was Daniel Keaton...'*

Out of the corner of his eye Thomas tried to interpret the look of his friend. He wondered, not without a hint of sincere regret, what thoughts were now stirring in his mind.

Daniel remained impassive, his eyes fixed on the images. Finally, many of the questions that had gripped him in the last few hours were being answered. Katrine Johnson's rambling sentences gained meaning and, in hindsight, suggested that the doctor, having received the card from her husband, did not have time to see that video before she was killed.

'The cloning solution, as I told you, was the last card Malcolm played. You developed into the physiological cloner, I took care of you day by day until your birth, if you can still call it that. Your mother and I were forced to welcome you into the family to take care of you, waiting for you to become what we already knew: a football phenomenon. Of course, cloning does not produce a photocopy of the cloned individual. In the absence of specific stimuli you could have become a tennis player, or maybe a basketball player. Or an individual with little interest in sport. Every man is a unique entity, Robert. You just had a predisposition, everything else had to be built. From an early age, therefore, you were welcomed into the Soccer Town school, where the best coaches and athletic trainers took care of you by amplifying your already innate sports skills. That's how you became "The King". As for the physical appearance, it was important not to leave traces of cloning. Daniel Keaton, or his family, or perhaps some too curious journalist might have noticed an excessive resemblance between

you. The risk was high. Aesthetically, social condition and life experience can have some influence, but what happens when two people live in similar environments? For these reasons, from the very beginning, Malcolm's money surgeons modified your facial features just enough to make you look less like Daniel Keaton. We often took advantage of some fortuitous event. Remember that time in junior high, a defender elbowed you in the chin? Here, we took the opportunity to operate on a bone reduction, and leave you in the hospital a few more days. Sinusitis? Through endoscopic surgery the problem was solved, but we took the opportunity to justify the rhinoplasty we gave you. I'm guessing Keaton got the same results medically, by corticosteroids. Sometimes nature anticipated us. The lower dental arch of your face was a bit protruding from the upper one, a slight defect that presumably Daniel Keaton never corrected, perhaps hiding it behind the beard. We acted immediately and later we talked about "postoperative therapy" to justify the botulinum injections, which we needed to intervene on the masseter muscle and reduce the width of the jaw. Luckily, you were surrounded by the best doctors on the square and in the end you never suspected a thing. It looked like the path of a young boy with some minor medical problem. No surprises, in short, except one: neither Malcolm nor I had foreseen that I could become attached to you and love you like a real son. You had to be, and you were, the most precious diamond among the many samples used solely to enrich the show and the Soccer Town boxes. I'm not talking about the show business, the game itself. I'm talking about the little theatre Malcolm put on. The whole world of football is a farce, Robert! It pains me to be the one to tell you this, but it's necessary if I want to save your life. I promised your mother moments before she left us because of her illness...'

Daniel struggled to swallow. He wasn't so sure he wanted to go through with it. Fortunately, the pressure of the report gave him no choice.

'*All Soccer Town games are piloted. You champions are kept in the dark so as not to upset your serenity and allow you to give your best. The collaboration of the players who have to suffer this charade, or decide to leave the league for lack of stimuli, or even worse to denounce the staging, is ensured by the biochip that have...*'

His voice suddenly broke. Although overwhelmed by pain and remorse, Dr Vincent Konnor ran almost immediately.

'*...that I have, with my team, installed in their brains. They believe they are only wearing the chip used for physical monitoring and data acquisition by the medical-statistical centre. In fact, each of them is grafted a biochip in the cerebral cortex, which allows Soccer Town's jailers to kill them at any time, splattering the brains of anyone who gets in the way. Unfortunately, sometimes the chip has been used. Thank God, only three times. In most cases they are kept quiet, from then on threatened players cooperate and are the first to sever relationships with family and friends, fearing retaliation. In this way they protect them from their torturers, but they also facilitate the final phase of the cruel Soccer Town project: forgetfulness.*'

Dr Konnor lowered his eyelids for a couple of seconds. He caught his breath, then continued his confession.

'*What none of them suspects to the last, unfortunately, is the end that will be reserved for them when they are no longer useful. At the end of their false career, through the biochip installed in the brain, the players are smemorised and literally abandoned in Hidden City. Here they will be left alive without identity until the last of their days. If only it were possible, Malcolm would not hesitate to eliminate them mercilessly, but it would rais too many suspicions. The chip implanted by the Registry Management on all citizens of the State would detect anomalous deaths in individuals like you players who, no longer suitable for high level competitive activity, are still young and in excellent health. Subsequent* enquiries may uncover the hinterland of Soccer Town. Officially, you champions enjoy a well-deserved post-career rest in the luxurious world of Soccer Eden. But Soccer Eden doesn't exist!'

Thomas turned to look for his friend's gaze. Fears about Jerry's fate also found worrying confirmation.

'Soccer Eden is just a facade invention, powered by fake videos, manipulated by experts. Players on leave are forced to register them before their minds are emptied. Although I have been a faithful servant of the organization, and I am ashamed of it, from the beginning of this bad story I have tried to make up for it. I tampered with the chip installed in your brain. It can never do you any harm. I did something for the other guys sent to Hidden City too. I saved their memories by inserting a virus into the Reset Machine, the forget-me-never machine, which instead of erasing the memories saved them. Those kids' lives are in Area 51. It's all stored on the Reset Machine chip. The recovery software is in there too. It seemed like the safest place to hide everything. In recent years, moreover, for greater security I have modified my virus, creating a neuronal superstructure that simulates the state of forgetfulness, ready to disappear at the first optical shock. It will be enough to bombard your eyes with a blinding flash of light to regain your memory. I used Müller's cell. It's a glial cell found in the retina. It participates in bidirectional communication with neurons and through the retinal layer, it reaches the internal segments of the photoreceptors. I have reprogrammed this cell to act as a switch as soon as the shock created by the flash of light creates a polarization excursion. I've been trying to send some clues to the police for about a year now, hoping someone will pick them up. I wasn't able to come out of the closet or leak much, because that would have meant signing my and your death sentence. The police are mostly corrupt. You never know who you're talking to, whether it's a Malcolm puppet or an honest cop. There's a big risk of ending up in the wolf's lair. After I record this video I'm *going to go to Malcolm and ask him to save you, because they've already decided to get you out of the way. If you're listening to me right now, that means my mission has failed. After all, only a few came out of the White Room alive. Try to keep yourself safe and save the memories of your colleagues. If they catch you, simulate forgetfulness, it'll be your last chance not to get killed. I altered Area 51's access system by entering your genetic data. This will allow you to get into the labs to retrieve those guys' memories. In this mem-chip you will find directions to pass all the controls and arrive undisturbed at my lab. There you'll find a monitor on. To access it you will need to enter the same code used to retrieve this chip. Once authenticated, it will show you the time and route to the Reset Machine. Its software is connected to the movement and laboratory management room, you can always move at the right time. You'll also find the password and processor needed to retrieve the memories, regardless of what security work my colleagues may have done on the machine. Simply type in your password at the end of the process. Parallel software will guide you through the transfer of memories.'*

The man breathed a sigh, by now his confession was coming to an end.

'As soon as the memories are backed up, the Reset Machine will automatically send an alarm signal to the security system. Unfortunately, I couldn't sabotage it and this was the obstacle that didn't allow me to take the memories and save them, before risking my fate with Simon Malcom. I'd have been a dead man after a few hours and I wouldn't have done anything. When you're in Area 51, don't trust anyone. Most of my colleagues are in Malcolm's pocket. Pay particular attention to Dr Vivian. It was she who eliminated the few who tried to rebel, and it is she who stimulates or indulges the most absurd ideas of that madman.'

One last sigh, finally the farewell.

'Forgive me for what I did and for keeping you in the dark.'

The video stopped abruptly a moment later. Maybe it was cut to hide his protagonist's emotional breakdown.

Daniel and Thomas crossed their eyes again. The first thought went to Josie.

'We have to warn Josie,' said Thomas, who was already dialling the number from his communicator's address book. Daniel waited. 'Damn it, she's unreachable! She may have her communicator disabled.'

'Let's leave her a video message.'

'Yes. I had already thought of that.'

Thomas started recording.

'Josie, leave Area 51 immediately. Dr Vivian is not the person you think she is. Don't trust her. You're in danger.'

Immediately afterwards he launched the file and turned to Daniel.

'Area 51?'

'Area 51. Let's just hope we get there in time.'

Daniel quickly programmed the Criton's autopilot and then turned off the monitor, in which Dr Konnor's proven face was still visible.

In an office in Area 51, another hand turned off its own video, fixed on the same image.

Chapter 36

'It was as we thought. There's no doubt about it now.'
'Are they still in your custody?'
'We don't let them out of our sight a moment. They'll probably catch up with her there, Captain.'
'At this point it was inevitable. Get ready, anything can happen.'
'Good news, Captain.'
On the other hand, the silence of the interlocutor demanded that he continued.
'We have recovered our subject. He's fine.'
'I was sure our medical team would have made miracles.'
'Over and out, Captain.'
'Over and out, Trenton.'

Chapter 37

The guard at the entrance was polite but firm. He was under strict orders to withdraw the communicators from anyone accessing the medical centre as a guest, and he had no intention of making exceptions.

Josie had insisted, making up a story about medical results that she was waiting with Dr Vivian, but the guard had been adamant despite verifying the authenticity of the appointment.

Anticipating this inconvenience, Josie had set up plan B: turn off the communicator, so that it would not be detected by the scanners, and give the guard a spare one.

Plan B had worked perfectly, and now Josie was pawning the elevator that would take her to the 238th floor by herself. The doors had already closed and the numbers on the display had started to scroll. She picked up the communicator, previously hidden in the inside pocket of her jacket, and activated it.

A loud sound confirmed the ignition. Immediately afterwards, another beep announced the presence of a video message on the answering machine. It was Thomas'.

'There will be news,' she said. She selected the message and gave her consent to receive it. After a few moments, Thomas' three-dimensional silhouette freed itself from the monitor, crystallizing into a still image. It only waited for the user's last consent to start registration.

It didn't come. A *jingle* of a few notes warned Josie that she had arrived at the selected floor.

'So soon,' she thought.

She took the audio off the communicator, closed the

message menu and put it inside her jacket just before the doors opened.

She had an unwelcome surprise waiting for her on the way out. Six feet tall, broad shoulders, shaved hair, infrared visor, uniform already seen on the ground floor guard.

The security man did not dwell on pleasantries.

'Dr Smith, please come out. Give me your communicator. You were told at the entrance, it seems to me, that you are not allowed to take it with you during your visit to our Medical Centre.'

So he pointed to the left side of the jacket with his head.

'What a fool,' Josie scolded herself, 'I should have known there were cameras in such a protected place.'

She had no other choice. She took the communicator out of her jacket and handed it over, without adding anything else.

Then she stepped to the right, but she got stuck. The man, while avoiding physical contact, obstructed her passage.

'I'm forced to escort you to the lobby, Dr Smith. This is the procedure for anyone who contravenes the security provisions. It's the orders. I'm sorry.'

'I understand,' just syllabled Josie, but a female voice interfered.

'It's all right, officer.'

She knew that voice.

'Dr Smith had my permission to take the communicator with her. We're waiting for the results of some important tests. Petty officer Hunter was not informed. It was an oversight on my part.'

Almost simultaneously, the officer was reading a similar notice on his service communicator.

'No problem, Dr Vivian.'

He handed the communicator back to Josie and apologized to her for the setback. Finally, he walked away.

'Thank you, Jennifer. You saved me a lot of hassle,' Josie said when she was free to speak.

'I saw you on my monitor trying to convince the first guard. I heard your little story to bring the communicator with you. Is it that important?'

'I'd say so. It's about why I came to see you. I need your help. I have things to check and ask you.'

'Let's go to my study, then. It'll be better to be quiet and mostly alone.'

'Thank you, Jennifer.'

'I'll lead the way.'

Jennifer Vivian was aware that she was very lucky, but this time events had evolved shamelessly in her favour, serving on a silver platter Josie Smith and perhaps some valuable information.

She always thought that luck helped the bold. Now she was sure.

CHAPTER 38

Waking up in the underground of Hidden City was the last thing he thought could happen to him. The room where he had just opened his eyes was the one where, after talking for hours with Jerry Crenna and his friend, he had fallen asleep the night before.

He could not return to his cover work immediately, he had to wait for the next period of shielding. Hence, that forced stop.

The artificial lights in the basement painted all the hours of the day in the same shade, but his communicator signaled that the night had already passed and the morning was almost over. He'd slept a lot unlike his habits.

Tony's thoughts automatically returned to the night before.

In so many years of career he had never heard a story that could even come close to the one that Jerry and the great champion Robert Konnor had told him.

If he had not seen with his own eyes the mythical "The King" relegated underground in Hidden City, he would have had many doubts about the authenticity of that story. A story that was incredible.

Robert had talked about the video his father left before Malcolm killed him, and how he tried to save himself and his wife. But he was captured before he could fully plan his escape. The only two things he was able to do in time were to warn his wife by voice mail and have her find the DNA card.

After that, events had precipitated. He was captured. Following his father's advice, he had pretended to have been smemorized and, like the others, he had been confined to Hidden City.

Finding out the truth that way had come as a shock to him. Every time he thought about it, he was attacked by anguish. The concern for his wife was also great. He couldn't tell her everything and ignored her fate. Tony didn't feel like telling him the news that he'd learned from watching the news...

Jerry had explained that Robert's arrival a few months earlier had been very important for the guys in Hidden City. Previously, only a few of them had recovered the memory in a fortuitous way, without understanding the mechanism. Then Robert had explained what his father had told him about the use of light flashes and so many of the newcomers had been *rememorized*.

Tony had been listening, greedy for the truth, almost all night before falling into a deep sleep.

His communicator now indicated the number of minutes left until the next shielding period. He got up and went to the adjoining room. There was Jerry and Robert, they were talking with glasses in their hands.

'Good morning, guys,' said Tony.

'Good morning,' replied Jerry.

'I hope that that kind of bed wasn't too uncomfortable,' Robert added, waving goodbye.

'I slept like a log.'

'We're celebrating the last of the recovered boys. Yesterday, two more regained their memories,' Jerry explained. 'Would you like some whiskey?'

'No, thank you. I don't drink alcohol.'

'I forgot that a transgressive guy like you only drinks the dangerous pear juice,' his fake co-worker ironically said.

'How many of you have regained your memory?' Tony

asked, ignoring the friendly provocation.
'Almost a hundred.'
'What about the others?'
'Their memories are still in Area 51.'
'But there are enough of us to get out of this place, blow up Soccer Town and help our friends,' Robert confidently intervened. 'We have two advantages on our side. They don't know we recovered the memory and they don't even suspect we can be armed.'
'Yes, I noticed it when you welcomed me...' Tony joked.
'During one of our searches underground in Hidden City, looking for hiding places and bases of operations, we found an arsenal. Probably hidden by the underworld and then abandoned during the global exodus from this part of the city. They're not the latest technology, but they still hurt.'
'When I walked in here, I saw you studying maps. Do you have something in mind?' Tony asked, showing off his reporter's instincts.
'We've been watching the movement of our jailers for months. Maybe we found a flaw in their system, thanks in part to Jerry who managed to infiltrate like Trevor among them. There is a strip of land in Hidden City that is not patrolled by M-Scouters, but remotely controlled by old infrared detectors. Our Trevor also managed to get himself included in the control room shifts, and discovered a bug in the software that manages the detection sensors.'
That's when Jerry stepped in.
'When infrared sensors record rapid temperature changes in a range exceeding twenty-four degrees Celsius, the software goes haywire. Since the climate is controlled artificially, large variations are unthinkable and therefore not foreseen in the software code. The programmer, however, has prudently inserted a routine on the possible error, which

involves resetting the sensors and the interface with the control unit. When that happens, our spy goes blind for 14 minutes.'

'I bet you found a way to reset it,' Tony said.

'Of course!' continued Jerry proudly. 'We have long had control of the old scientific institute of the university. The disorganized and senseless depopulation of Hidden City in the years leading up to New Day, many years later, has served our cause. We've taken possession of a great deal of equipment and scientific material. Among them a large supply of liquid nitrogen. We studied a lot and we got something out of it. Of course, we can't improvise as electronics or chemistry experts, we have spent our lives on an artificial turf field, but the willingness to get out of here has helped us a lot. Sometimes we wonder if we would not have obtained equally surprising results by continuing our studies. Someone among us, at least. Surely we are not imbeciles as they paint us, on the other hand, even a dull passage or a lob at the right time are acts that denote a form of intelligence.'

Tony then asked the question that Robert and Jerry had been expecting from the beginning.

'Only there's one problem that's still holding you back. Right? Otherwise you'd be out of this hell already.'

'In fact, there are two problems,' replied Robert. 'The first is to arrive, without getting caught, at the nearest sensor to give it a nice shower of liquid nitrogen at minus one hundred and eighty degrees. If we don't come up with something, they'll intercept us first.'

'This problem could be overcome. *Trevor* could take care of that at the control centre,' Jerry objected.

'No way. We've been over this a thousand times. Come on. You'd be signing your own death warrant, which is why there are two problems. Vigilantes are always organized in pairs, you would be forced to eliminate your partner and his disappearance could not be hidden for more than a few minutes. We have to find another system. Regardless, the biggest problem is the second. Fourteen minutes aren't enough time to get out of Hidden City and we can't crash the system twice in a row. We'd arouse too manysuspicions, those bastards would send their M-Scooters out on a killing spree.'

'It would take at least twenty-four to twenty-five minutes to get out of this shitty place,' Jerry added.

'How do you plan to solve the problem, then?'

'We would like to create an intermediate foothold in our escape route, using some heat shields we found at the university. With this shielding, the sensors shouldn't detect us,' Jerry said. 'During the first tilt of the software, we would have to reach this point, and then escape for the next fourteen minutes.'

Robert turned his back forty-five degrees and pointed his index finger at a point on the map.

'We're thinking of building our bridge base here.'

'How come you don't use the heat shields to escape directly?' Tony asked again.

'Good question. We've thought about it several times, but shields wouldn't be enough for everyone and, above all, they wouldn't give us the absolute certainty of escaping infrared. It is very difficult to reproduce the outside temperature on the shields, certainly the software would detect a small spot of lighter or darker colour on the move. The large heat shield that we are going to form, instead, will be seen only as a large spot of colour barely different from the adjacent colours, but still. It would be mistaken for any limestone area in the area, or something like that. We expect the construction of the foothold to take about a month. We've programmed an average of three or four computer tilts per week to allow our guys to transport the shields and mount them.'

'Sounds like a well thought-out plan,' complimented the journalist.

'Glad to hear you say that. As soon as we find a way to get to the sensors, we'll go with the operation.'

'Maybe I could make myself useful,' Tony said. Robert and Jerry remained silent. 'If we could get Jerry and me to pair up, we'd be done. Don't forget, I'm a vigilante too.'

'I've made a few friends lately and it shouldn't be hard to get you on the M-Scooter team. We can work on that,' Jerry said.

'Fine! I hope all this turns out to be superfluous anyway. An associate of mine should be out of Old Town by now. As soon as Thomas gets my message...'

Robert and Jerry's eyes crossed again. This time, though, they stayed low. Tony understood.

'Do you know something about Brandon that I don't?'

Robert breathed a long sigh before answering.

'He almost made it...'

Tony kept quiet. The guilt stopped his breathing for a moment.

'How did it happen?' he asked, his eyes already clear, his voice trembling.

'He was intercepted by two M-Scooters and there was no escape for him. I'm sorry.'

Tony's pain imposed silence. The journalist walked away in an adjacent alley and disappeared from sight for a few minutes. When he went back over the arch, his eyes were dry and he had a tangible desire for revenge. Jerry read it in her eyes.

'Tony...maybe you and Trevor better get back to work,' Robert encouraged him. 'In a few minutes we'll have the next shielding period. If you were to skip this, an absence too long might arouse suspicion.'

They both nodded, without objecting. Jerry gave his friend a pat and a whisper of "courage!" Then they moved away in the direction of the platform they used as an elevator.

Robert went back to his papers instead. He was busy rearranging thoughts and maps, a few seconds later, when the beep of the speakerphone made its way into the quiet of the basement. A voice cracked in agitation.

'Alarm! They've got us surrounded! They're up there.'

Robert moved into the next room, where other comrades controlled the environment on the surface. He was met by Mark, once defender of the Miranda Concept Team and now in charge of the control room.

'It's over, Robert. They're up there. I don't know how they did it, but they found us.'

'Let's stay calm, Mark. They can guess where we are but they only have one door available: the lift. For the time being, we'll just have to keep it closed...'

He left the room and attacked the dark gully that served as a hallway to the various rooms, leading to the mobile platform. He ran like the old days, Robert Konnor.

'Jerry and Tony are going straight into the wolf's lair,' he thought desperately. In a few seconds, he devoured the metres that separated him from the environment in which the lift was accessed. The closed doors revealed the ineffectiveness of his attempt. The control panel indicated minus fourteen. Jerry and Tony were already on their way up.

Mark's voice came out of the communicator again.

'Robert! They're right on top of the lift and someone's using it.'

Minus nine.

'I know, unfortunately. It's Jerry and Tony. I didn't have time to stop them.'
A break.
'I'm sorry...' hissed sadly.
Minus five.
'We don't stand a chance anymore, guys...'
Minus three.
He fell to the ground.
Minus two.
The King stood still. One thought occupied his mind and said it was over forever.
Minus one.
Earth.

CHAPTER 39

ALLOWED ACCESS

The last DNA scanner was passed.

Now Thomas and Daniel were inside Vincent Konnor's studio. The indications given by the scientist had been impeccable and had allowed the two of them to enter Area 51 without being conspicuous.

At least that's what they thought.

As Dr Konnor indicated, they had left the Criton in the staff parking area and used Transport Sphere number twenty-four to reach the most isolated area of the laboratories.

The path that had led them to the studio of the luminary was dotted with automatic checkpoints, located at the entrance to each passageway. Obviously, everything had gone smoothly.

Dr Konnor's office was large and divided into two zones. The smaller one was occupied by a desk and an armchair, one wall bore the honours, degrees, awards and recognitions obtained by the scientist. The largest area was occupied by analysing machines and other technological devices, equipment that the two had never seen before in their lives.

These were certainly sophisticated and advanced versions of known instrumentation, if not even prototypes still unknown to the scientific community.

All workstations were equipped with holo-consoles and monitors and were aligned in three rows, creating, in fact, as many corridors. The lights above the equipment were off, except for one.

In the semi-darkness of the third corridor a faint glow

attracted the attention of the two. It must have been the monitor Dr Konnor indicated.

Daniel took a couple of steps forward and approached the lighted post.

'Here we go. This is it.'

'Go with yet another DNA analysis,' his friend urged him.

Daniel put his hand on the compartment. As expected, the monitor claimed his password. He typed the letters of his name like this once again.

A flashing sign appeared:

THE PASSWORD OF THE RESET MACHINE IS
'FORGIVENESS'
THE ACCESS CHIP IS BELOW

The intermittence of the message was synchronized with the numbers of a short countdown. At the bottom of the monitor a tongue of space had been freed and a chip of almost non-existent thickness had escaped. Daniel grabbed him and waited for the countdown to reach his goal.

Zero.

Now the monitor was occupied by miniatures of the main areas controlled by the CCTV system. The software designed by Dr Konnor indicated in four minutes and twenty-five seconds the first useful moment to venture into the maze of Area 51 and reach the Reset Machine. For the next one they would have to wait two hours and fifty-seven minutes.

A hand movement on the word CONNECT put Dr Konnor's computer on line with Daniel's communicator.

A timid beep confirmed the connection.

'You keep it,' Daniel said, handing his friend the jewel of microcircuits he just recovered. 'The same person better not keep both chips in case we get intercepted.'

Thomas nodded.

'Once the memories are taken, we'll have security on our backs. Remember Konnor's warning?'

'Our situation is a little different,' Thomas objected. 'Dr Konnor said he'd be a dead man after a few hours, but only because those criminals at Area 51 knew he was the only one who could tamper with the Reset Machine. We, on the other hand, are complete strangers. We'll have plenty of time to get away, don't worry. A guy as precise as he would have warned his son, otherwise.'

'Okay. You're right but...I'm nervous!'

His friend comforted him with a smile.

'I'm not used to handling this much adrenaline anymore,' Daniel explained.

'Everything will be all right, don't worry,' repeated Thomas. 'Dr Konnor, as you can see, has thought of everything. He didn't let...'

'Look at this!' Daniel interrupted him, shaking his head nervously.

One of the miniatures on the monitor included a familiar face among its protagonists.

Daniel activated the console and selected the image. This one got bigger, taking up all the available space.

'I knew it was dangerous to come here. I had to stop her!' he looked angrily, and equally concerned.

'She may have asked a few too many questions,' Thomas remarked.

'We simply didn't have time to warn her. We must save her.'

'I care about her as much as you do, Daniel. But we have priorities. Josie would agree with me too.'

The scene on the monitor depicted Josie Smith in the company of a man pointing a gun at her, forcing her to walk through an open door.

Daniel began to move the controls in search of other images to follow his friend. She seemed to have disappeared into thin air. The room she entered was obviously unmonitored.

Meanwhile, time had flown by and barely 53 seconds were missing.

'Let's not panic,' Thomas urged him. 'We need to get those guys' memories back. Then we'll take care of Josie and notify the police.'

Daniel remained silent and with his head still bent over the console he looked up towards the upper left corner. Thirteen seconds left to leave that place.

He activated the communicator, which gave the first indication of the route to follow.

EXIT ON THE LEFT
TAKE CORRIDOR H

Daniel put his hand near the door sensor. It opened. The two of them turned left and after a few steps they took the right corridor. The communicator indicated to continue for another fifty metres. In the short journey the two passed five crossroads, without meeting a soul.

The plan of Area 51 was a perfect chessboard that drew its lines with morbid symmetry, and made any intersection between one corridor and another equal.

A purple flashing sign blocked them a few meters before the umpteenth crossroads.

STOP
LEAN ON THE LEFT SIDE

They followed orders. From the hallway that intersected theirs came a rumour.

Thomas and Daniel stood still, and almost breathless. The voices became louder and louder, bouncing from one side of the walls to the other. Daniel began to doubt the effectiveness of Konnor's system.

The image provided by the communicator was of a guy in a white coat followed by two clusters of muscles in red uniforms. The little band of men were a few feet from them. The sound of footsteps stopped. The hiss of a door opening replaced those sounds for a moment.

The three men entered and disappeared quickly leaving the door behind them, which closed a moment later.

Daniel felt almost guilty for doubting a scientist like Vincent Konnor.

The communicator light turned green again. The message had changed.

FORWARD
AT THE FIRST INTERSECTION TURN RIGHT

The two followed the directions to the letter, entering a corridor identical to the others. They went on for another 20 metres.

DESTINATION REACHED ON THE RIGHT

The new message caught Daniel almost unprepared. He stopped suddenly. Thomas did the same.

Between them and the Reset Machine was the usual DNA-scanner. Daniel offered the palm of his hand to yet another chamber.

Access to the lab was unlocked. The two friends hurried in.

A moment later, the door closed.

CHAPTER 40

'He's on the line.'

'Just him?' Torst said just to gain time and try to figure out the value of that call in advance.

'Yes. That's the one. Straight from the White Room.'

'Put him on!'

After a few moments of silence, the outline of Julian Preston was drawn by the communicator.

'We've got two nosy guys in Area 51. I want you to take care of this personally, quickly and above all, definitively.'

'I was already on it. Gideon and I just walked into the labs, and we're on our way to surprise those two snoopers.'

'The Smith?'

'Dr Vivian already took care of it. She won't ask any more inappropriate questions.'

'I hope forever.'

The innuendo was clear.

'We'll do it as soon as we've thought about her two friends, too. She's already somewhere safe. Maybe the morgue will give them the group discount.'

For that joke, on the other hand, there was no sign of appreciation. The Chief liked to flaunt his own sarcasm, he didn't tolerate other people's sarcasm because it could cloud his presence, his ego.

Torst understood, but he didn't care. The fact that hr didn't hurt Preston's susceptibility was already a good sign. He was freeing himself from the state of total subordination, even verbal, which characterized anyone who came into contact with the tenant of the most famous room in Soccer Town.

'How did they get in?'

'We don't know yet, but we will find out. We'll get them to tell us. It will be my cure, then, to reward them with a few more seconds of life.'

'Where are they now?'

'In the smemorization lab.'

'Please welcome them.'

'It will be done.'

Chapter 41

The laboratory in which Thomas and Daniel were located was identical to Vincent Konnor's, and to all the others that made up Area 51, with the difference that it housed only two rows of scientific equipment and, above all, the Reset Machine, the brain eater, the smemorization machine. It was there, proud of its cold cruelty.

'This is it,' said Thomas with one hand on Daniel's shoulder.

'Let us proceed.'

Daniel moved a few steps forward and headed towards the central part of the lab. His shadow, pallidly illuminated by the low light, as he followed him, became loose.

As he passed the first row of stations, he noticed that part of the laboratory was occupied by a long, narrow, transparent parallelepiped. The inscription placed on the lower part of the fairing left no room for conjecture as to its purpose:

CLONING INCUBATOR

'That's where they created Robert Konnor with my DNA,' thought Daniel.

Thomas saw in his eyes the shadow of uncertainty.

'It feels weird, doesn't it?' he asked.

Daniel waited a moment. Then he nodded.

He wondered if Robert Konnor had ever met his real mother, made of chips and titanium, a patient cell packer. Most likely, he never made it to his father's lab because he'd been captured before. He had almost certainly observed, however, the dramatic video stored in the Union Bank. The information that the two friends had acquired up to that point confirmed this hypothesis.

The intuition gained in the bank vault could be considered, by now, a certainty. The first access to the safe deposit box was to be attributed to his father Vincent, who had deposited the mem-chip before going to Malcolm. The other two were attributable to Robert, who had taken the memory and then put it back in its place, just long enough to discover the bitter truth.

'I wonder what happened to Robert Konnor,' thought Daniel. If one day he had met him, what emotional reaction would he have had when confronted with a person who possessed the same genetic inheritance as his? And how would he have considered him, how would he call him? A twin brother who is 29 years younger? Or himself catapulted back in time?

Maybe just another person.

The reset machine, apparently, looked like a tube three and a half metres high and with a circumference of about six. At mid-height, a deep recess revealed an opening that divided it in two. At the bottom left, a section of the cladding was occupied by a monitor in the outer frame of which was the chip housing.

Thomas set it up in the required spot. An inscription and a scroll bar appeared on the monitor:

FILE TRANSFER ACTIVATED

The scroll bar had just started to turn dark blue. The inches of white indicated the waiting time, and it seemed endless.

On one non-visible side of the laboratory another door opened, leaving room for the silent and elongated shadow of two silhouettes.

'How do you think we can find Josie?' Daniel suddenly asked.

'We have to try Dr Konnor's closed circuit. If that doesn't

work, the only alternative we have is to go to the police,' Thomas replied.

'We could use our chip as a bargaining chip to get Josie to deliver us.'

'You don't want to screw up the whole operation, I hope. She'd never let you do that herself.'

'I didn't really mean it. We could bluff.'

'Are you crazy? It's too dangerous. Those are people who don't mess around.'

'Your friend is right, Professor Keaton. Listen to him. We don't feel like joking at all.'

Daniel and Thomas turned around. A red dot moved from their backs to their chests. Two men with guns were threatening them.

'Put your hands up and come forward slowly,' intimated one of them. Daniel recognized him on the fly.

'Listen to this...' Thomas tried to buy time, but it was Daniel who silenced him.

'Forget it, there's nothing a dirty cop can understand.'

Thomas was surprised that his friend knew the man.

'I'm glad to see you remember me, Professor Keaton,' replied Detective Torst. He had an ironic smile on his face and a big backpack on his shoulders.

'I didn't trust you from the very first moment,' Daniel confessed, looking at him with disgust. 'What did you do to Katrine Johnson and Josie Smith?'

'These are matters that do not concern you,' replied Torst, shaking his head to the right at the same time. The second man understood and approached Daniel by grabbing his wrists. 'I advise you not to resist, it will be easier for everyone. Believe me.'

Neither friend found the strength to replicate anything. They were trapped by now.

'Gideon, give it an extra squeeze from me.'

Daniel had his wrists locked behind his back. As he turned around, he peeked at the scroll bar on the monitor, hoping that the two guys hadn't noticed. Blue had already invaded three-quarters of white. He moved a few inches to obscure their field of vision. Thomas understood his friend's intentions and, pretending to have given in, advanced a few steps and went to Gideon to get his wrists locked in turn.

'I'm pleased with this sudden desire to cooperate,' Torst commented in the usual tone of mockery.

Gideon finished his work.

'Turn around!'

The two of them obeyed without a word, turning their backs on the torturers.

The darkness suddenly attacked their eyes. On Daniel and Thomas' heads now stood out two full face helmets, used for virtual reality.

Torst continued his sarcastic theatrics.

'I hope you have no objection to seeing your path only as we like.'

The eyes of the two hostages had just become accustomed to the darkness when the helmet's internal monitor came to life and gave them an artefact view of their surroundings.

In the virtualized world, the lab had shrunk and emptied. A monotonous white monopolized the walls. The openings had disappeared, the corridors and intersections between them had multiplied.

The aim was to disorient the two hostages, making them lose any possible reference points.

'Walk!' Torst ordered.

Daniel and Thomas moved, following a virtual arrow.

Suddenly, a sign appeared before their eyes.

Daniel couldn't believe it.

'What if this is just another trick?' he asked himself.

He instinctively turned in Thomas' direction. He found only a void, perfect candour, even though he knew his friend was beside him.

He took a deep breath and reread those words.

Chapter 42

The lit display had stopped at zero, but the hatch had not opened.

'What's going on?' Tony asked himself out loud.

'I don't know, it never happened,' Jerry replied.

The answer came from the intercom.

'We've been discovered. We're trapped.'

Jerry immediately recognized Mark's voice.

'Where are they?'

'Over your heads. I was able to stop the hatch from opening at the last minute, or else you would have met them already.'

'Maybe they followed you here,' commented Robert from forty metres deep, to whom Mark's trick had given his face colour back, but only for a short time.

'I don't think so. I was more careful than usual. There's no way we could have been followed,' Jerry replied.

'The point is not to understand how they found us, but to solve the problem,' Tony intervened, the first to regain sufficient lucidity to deal with the emergency.

'We'll figure something out when we get back down,' Jerry said when he activated the descent control.

Nothing.

He tried again. All stopped, the lift wouldn't pop.

'What's going on, Mark? I can't get down. Can you do it from down there?' Jerry asked.

'Unfortunately, no. I'm sorry.'

'What do you mean "no"?'

'I managed to block the hatch, but too late. The opening signal had already started. I blocked it by disconnecting the power supply to the control units and, therefore, as soon as it is restored, the hatch will necessarily have to complete the opening. Until the sequence is completed, I cannot enter any more commands.'

'What's this story?' Tony asked in amazement.

'The lift is operated by old sequential control units that were used in the last century,' Mark explained. 'A few months ago we had a similar problem.'

'The only thing we can do is wait,' admitted Robert's voice, back in possession of the intercom. 'You must stay there until they're gone.'

'Not really.' replied Mark, the voice full of bitterness.

'More surprises? What's the problem now?' Robert blurted out.

Jerry tried to ease the tension.

'Guys, let's not panic. We don't get anything out of it. We just have to keep our heads. Talk, Mark. What did you want to say?'

'The elevator's safety system provides for the automatic, unmanageable activation of an auxiliary generator after a ten-minute blackout.'

Jerry easily came to the conclusion.

'You mean in less than ten minutes the hatch will open?'

'That's right. Precisely six minutes and forty-four seconds from now.'

'Damn it! Mark, can you tell me how many of those bastards there are and if there are any outside the hangar?'

'Of course. I can see them from the infrared sensors. There are ten of them and they're all alone. They're all inside the hangar.'

'That's what I was hoping you'd say. We have a chance, guys.'

The silence of the other three was more eloquent than

any exhortation. Jerry laid out his plan.

'If, as I think, the vigilantes over our heads didn't find us by following Tony and me but found us by accident, we have a one in two chance they know our location but haven't reported it to headquarters yet. They don't know we're down here.'

Robert thought that this circumstance changed little, but he didn't want to intervene because he had extreme confidence in Jerry and was sure that his friend's arguments would come together in a precise plan.

'If we could neutralize them, we'd have a chance to maintain cover of our safe house.'

'It's impossible for two of you to neutralize ten of them. They're armed to the teeth,' Mark said.

Jerry shook his head.

'The hatch has a resistance of two kilotons and I have a bomb that will make everything disappear within a hundred meters. I've always taken it with me for extreme situations. This is an extreme situation.'

Quiet.

Robert and the others now understood.

'There has to be another solution,' said Tony, who when he left with Brandon on that journalistic mission never thought he'd end up like that.

'We have no choice, Tony. I'm sorry to drag you into this mess, but really, we have no alternative. You and I are two dead men no matter what. If these bastards haven't told our position yet, though, we'll have a chance to save the others and let them hope to make it one day.'

Mark's voice echoed again from the intercom.

'You only have a minute.'

'There's got to be another solution,' Robert repeated inside, but no idea came out of his mind.

Jerry put his hand in the pocket of his left leg and grabbed the bomb without taking it out. With his thumb he snapped the trigger guard and identified the slight recess into which he would have to insert his index finger to operate the micro-detonator.

He put it in.

Tony understood, but he didn't say a word.

Jerry kept his head down. His breathing got faster, as if a boulder was compressing his chest.

From the intercom came absolute silence, even though communication was open.

Mark checked his stopwatch. Two seconds left. He tried to cross Robert's eyes, but this was fixed on the closed lift doors. A distant and deaf noise signalled that the auxiliary generator had come to life to take it away from the two companions.

Robert closed his eyes.

At level zero, the hatch began to open.

CHAPTER 43

Having your head out of those helmets was a great relief. Being forcibly locked up in a false reality with deliberately faded outlines, it caused a feeling of bewilderment and suffocation at the same time.

The reality they found, once free from the game of the virtual, was however the same: prisoners at gunpoint.

'As you can see, Professor Keaton, I'm not that bad,' said Torst, who continued to hold them at gunpoint while Gideon freed them from the handcuffs. 'With their hands tied I think few would believe an accident,' he added with the usual ration of sarcasm.

Thomas slid his gaze over the walls to try to visualize where they were. It was an empty room with only two entrances. He wondered if at least one of them might come in handy, in the unlikely event that he and Daniel had turned the situation to their advantage.

Torst sensed the journalist's intentions.

'Mr Lewton, the entrance to this room is protected by a mixed biometric security system. Even if you kill me, you could never get out of here without my consent. The room is shielded and suitable for my purpose, otherwise I wouldn't have given you the tour of the labs.'

Thomas, as a keen observer, noticed that Torst had spoken of "entrance" to the singular. So one of the two openings didn't give on the labs.

'Do what you have to do and end this charade, Torst. What's your point?' Daniel blurted out.

'Don't be touchy, Professor, or I might change my mind and deny you my parting gift.'

Daniel did not respond to the provocation. He looked out of the corner of his eye to see if Thomas had something on his mind.

He didn't read anything.

He looked at his hands, in case he wanted to communicate something with his "talking fingers".

Nothing.

Torst resumed his monologue.

'I feel good today, so I've decided to let you die in sweet company.'

Gideon activated a command from his communicator. One of the two openings slid up. Streams of light quickly invaded the hidden environment, turning darkness into semi-darkness and letting the indistinct contours of a silent silhouette huddled on the ground emerge.

Daniel's heart skips a beat.

'I hope the gift is appreciated,' continued Torst, leaving his heavy backpack in a corner. The figure had already risen and was advancing towards them.

'Josie! What did they do to you?' Daniel asked, going to meet her in turn.

'Don't worry, I'm fine,' replied her friend.

Daniel instinctively laid his hands on her arms, as if he wanted to make sure that it was her and that she was in one piece. Josie's eyes, tired and frightened, could hardly get used to the light. They were a little red. Maybe she cried. She was taken by surprise when she felt Daniel's hand quickly reach over her shoulder and grasp her hand firmly. With great naturalness, he twisted his fingers around his friend's fingers and suddenly all the years that had been inserted into their lives seemed to disappear into thin air.

Torst's voice suddenly swooped over those present, like a boulder, taking everyone by surprise.

'Goodbye, gentlemen.'

His arm stretched out even more and his index finger slipped on the trigger.

Thomas' gaze crossed Gideon's sneer, who pointed his gun at him and approached Torst's left.

The latter took two steps back and pointed in the same direction.

Thomas understood. Now he knew who the man was. With a feline snap, he threw himself to the right, towards the exit.

The sights of the two weapons also followed the same direction.

A fiery red glow gave shape to a blade of light.

Quiet.

A deaf thud.

Chapter 44

'Don't worry, he's just stunned. When I can, I prefer not to kill people. After all, he's just a fool in Malcolm's pocket.'

Gideon's paralyzed body was lying on the ground near Thomas' feet.

'I was afraid you wouldn't believe my message. Luckily you believed me,' said Torst after retrieving the backpack. He thought it might be a hindrance when he fired, so he took it off.

'We had no alternative and there was nothing left to lose,' replied Thomas.

Daniel thought about the message that had appeared before his eyes while wearing the virtual reality helmet.

JUMP TO THE EXIT WHEN I TAKE TWO STEPS BACK.

The reference to the room shielding was also a clue.

'A real undercover cop pretending to be a dirty undercover,' he thought. He had a skilled double agent in front of him who, fortunately, was on the right side: theirs.

Daniel's face had regained its natural colour. He began to speak.

'I'm sorry I called you "dirty", Detective.'

'To take undeserved insults is the fate of all infiltrators. No problem, Professor,' Torst reassured him. 'Now all we have to think about is getting out of here, and fast. Gideon's biometric chip will have reported paralysis by now, so in a few minutes we'll have the entire Area 51 on our tail.'

'We should go back to the lab first,' replied Daniel.

'Of course. It was already accounted for. Those guys' memories are precious to me too.'

'Do you know this too?' Thomas asked.

'We know all about you. We have been following the case for several months, ever since Dr Vincent Konnor sent us some warning signals, fortunately received by the right people. It is from Dr Johnson's mansion that the shadow of my team is upon you, Professor Keaton.'

Daniel would have wanted to ask which side the small group of paramilitaries who had kept him company at Villa Konnor were on, but it was no use satisfying such curiosity. He preferred to ask a different question.

'Who killed Dr Johnson? You, Detective Torst, were at the university that day. I remembered it when you came to question me. We bumped into each other in the lobby.'

'Yes, I remember. Dr Johnson isn't dead. She's been taken over by my team and she's out of danger. It was Gideon who neutralized her. I didn't get to the university on time, but luckily it wasn't even too late to save her.'

'Personally, I never believed in suicide,' confirmed Daniel. Torst continued.

'We also know about Vincent Konnor's video. We saw it together, you in the Criton and me on my monitor. A bug has been installed on your car, Professor, as soon as this story is over we'll clean it up ourselves.'

'What about the Hidden City guys? How do you plan to proceed to save them?' Thomas asked, returning to the priority aspects of the matter.

'They're probably safe by now. One of my teams has taken control of the area and neutralized the vigilantes. Now they are searching for the shelter, the riot group is hiding in the basement.'

'Riot group?' Josie said out loud.

'Yes, Dr Smith. The flaw created by Dr Konnor in the smemorization system has borne fruit. It has allowed many to regain their memory and organize a clandestine resistance. Also why we're having difficulty locating them, but not for long.'

'You said you neutralized the vigilantes. What do you mean?' asked Thomas concerned.

'We didn't kill them, if that's what you mean. I told you, when I can avoid, I avoid it. We know about your colleagues Tony Stantford and Brandon Bolton, however,' Torst cut short. 'We assume that Stantford has made contact with the insurgents, but we have not heard from him for several hours. -Bolton, on the other hand, didn't make it. We were too late this time. I'm very sorry about your associate.'

The words Thomas would have wanted to add died on his lips. He turned his suffering gaze in another direction, merely nodding. In due course, he would vent his pain, under the right circumstances and with the right people. In front of a stranger he preferred to hide his torment.

Josie hugged him, Daniel just took a comforting pat. He'd never been good at expressing those feelings.

Torst took a thermal mini scanner from his pocket and put it near the door console. Red fingerprints appeared on the monitor.

'For security reasons, the door can only be opened by the person who closed it, and unfortunately Gideon closed it,' explained Torst. 'Anyway, it's not a problem, I'd also considered that possibility. We'll just need the heat trace left by his fingertips to get the combination,' he continued.

The red of the four prints appeared in different shades depending on the number pressed. The darker one belonged to the five, followed by the three, the nine and the eight. The sequence returned the order in which the four keys had been touched: the temperature of the finger, meeting a colder surface than the hand, decreased very little with each contact, leaving a less marked thermal trace.

The policeman typed on the 5398 keypad. The optical sensor lit up.

'I need your help now, Lewton,' Torst said. 'We need to give Mr Gideon a good eye examination. Will you help me lift him?'

It was clear to everyone that to get out you had to complete the procedure by scanning that man's iris. Unconscious, Gideon weighed at least twice as much. Thomas grabbed him by running his arm around his neck and inserting his shoulder from below. Torst did the same.

They brought his face closer to the sensor. With the other hand, Torst raised the man's eyelid, uncovering his eye. The eye scanner was satisfied. The door opened.

The two of them laid Gideon's body to the ground.

'Everybody out, quick. This way,' Torst said on leaving the room.

The first to follow him was Thomas, then Josie and Daniel who were still holding hands. He only trained the grip for a moment, time to check the communicator. Vincent Konnor's monitoring system had picked up the signal.

'You don't need your navigator, Professor Keaton. I know how to get to the Reset Machine. I'll lead the way.'

Torst accelerated his pace in spite of the size of the backpack, and took the corridor on the right. It was empty. The other three followed him.

They passed four crossroads and then turned left. Daniel kept an eye on the images in Dr Konnor's software. Not a soul around.

'Detective Torst, I'm not a cop, but it doesn't seem normal that it's all deserted,' commented Daniel worried.

'You're right, Professor. I noticed it myself, even before we caught you. This can't be good.'

A deafening clangour violently ended the conversation. The floor creaked under their feet, and a wide, deep crack opened up a few yards ahead.

Almost simultaneously, Detective Torst's communicator lit up. After activating it, a soldier's face took shape in miniature above his display.

That was Lieutenant Summer. The orders were clear: no calls during the stopover in Area 51 and his assistant would never violate the orders except for a very serious reason.

'Captain, you've been discovered. Your cover's blown and they're trying to destroy Area 51 with you inside.'

'Unfortunately, we just realized, Summer.'

'We're covering you from the east side, from there you can escape into the suburbs of Soccer Town. You will find access to the Transport Sphere. Hurry, though, we won't be able to secure a shield of fire for very long.'

'Were you able to access the White Room?' Torst asked.

'Not yet. In any case, unfortunately, its tenant is already running away.'

Next to the image of Lieutenant Summer appeared those of Simon Malcom and Jennifer Vivian fleeing, protected by bodyguards, aboard a vehicle.

'Hidden City?'

'Mission accomplished, Captain. Lieutenant Trenton located the guys. They're on their way.'

'Great. At least we needed good news.'

Torst turned to his fellow escapees to clarify the point

'Hidden City is under our control.'

'Over and out, Captain.'

'Over and out, Lieutenant.'

Another explosion thundered over their heads within seconds. Part of the ceiling came off, but it was dangling.

'Area 51 was built with special materials,' Torst revealed.

'Malcolm's no fool, but he certainly didn't expect all this technology to one day make it easier on his enemies. It will give us a little more time, even if sooner or later the structure will still give in. We have to split up at this point. One of us will go to retrieve the memory chip, the others will have to get to the suburbs.'

'I'll go!' Daniel immediately proposed.

'No, I'll take care of getting the chip back. But I'll need the password, Professor,' replied Torst, who implicitly understood himself with the words "one of us".

'I'll go!' said Daniel. He'd have felt more comfortable if the cop had got Thomas and Josie to safety.

Torst recorded the resoluteness with which Daniel had cancelled any margin for negotiation. He hoped that the decision was not due to any further reservations he had about him. It only took one look at him to realize he was just defending his friends.

'As you wish,' complied. 'We'll meet at Transport Sphere.'

Daniel squeezed Josie's hand tightly, then snapped her without looking her in the eye. He selected some options on his communicator and started running, then turned abruptly to the left.

Josie was petrified, her hand still steady in the position Daniel had left it.

The sound of Detective Torst's words brought her back down.

'Gentlemen, we have to go.'

CHAPTER 45

He did not know why, mysterious intuition or external intervention, supernatural or not, his index finger had not pressed the micro detonator trigger.

He didn't realize the time he was stuck. Surely it had been enough not to blow up, and not only metaphorically, the unexpected possibility of salvation. The fate of him and his companions had been linked, for a few moments, to his reflexes.

Once the hatch opened and reached the alignment between platform and ground, Jerry had not triggered the bomb and gave Lieutenant Trenton a chance to explain who they were and who they were looking for.

Jerry and Tony had remained impassive and, considering unlikely what the military was trying to make them believe, had also considered the hypothesis that it could be a trap to gain their trust and then get to the others.

Trenton had managed to break through the more than understandable wall of suspicion, disarming himself and sliding his weapon to their feet.

Jerry, to make sure it wasn't fake, had aimed down and pulled the trigger. A bar of light had cut through the air and dissolved in the furrow dug into the ground. Lieutenant Trenton's raised fist had previously blocked any reaction from his men.

To remove the last remnants of distrust that still separated him from the footballer and the journalist, the military had mentioned the rescue code, Daniel, Robert, Dr Vincent Konnor, his video and the method to recover the memories of the smemorized guys.

'This battle has also been won,' thought the lieutenant, now relieved.

'You're a tough guy to convince, Mr Crenna. But I finally made it,' said Trenton. 'I can't blame you, though. If I were you, I would have done exactly the same thing.'

Tony, as a good journalist, wanted to ask a thousand questions, but he understood very well that it was not the time.

Jerry put the safety back on the device he was still holding and grabbed the intercom.

'Robert, we have news!'

'We heard everything, Jerry. We too have been on edge, but finally our nightmare is over.'

'We have enough guns to go along with you,' Jerry said. 'I think you will need some help neutralizing the vigilantes.'

'That won't be necessary. They're all already under our control.'

Jerry felt he was freed from a huge burden.

Tony thought angrily of those who had overcome a thousand battles but not the last, and only for a breath: Brandon. 'It was my fault' repeated himself. A moment later, his rational side reminded him that he had driven Brandon away to protect him, and that to do so he had taken all the risks associated with his blind date with Dick Trevor.

He tried to chase that thought away, but he couldn't. Probably would have accompanied him for life.

Forty metres below Mark had already gathered the other guys.

'Here we go, Robert!'

'Is everybody here?'

'Yes!'

'Back to life. Let's get out of this place.'

CHAPTER 46

For the second time, the Reset Machine was ahead of him. On the monitor the scroll bar had already completed its course, the blue had swallowed up all the white who knows how long.

Luckily, that lab was in an internal area and Malcolm's bombs hadn't reached it yet.

A dialog box waited for user intervention and demanded the password.

Daniel typed FORGIVENESS. Just one word, but full of meaning. He thought for a moment about the psychological torment that had plagued Vincent Konnor's conscience during those years.

Torn apart by remorse for having endorsed such a wicked operation, Vincent had found a son in the midst of such cynicism, an idea always discarded in order not to compromise his scientific career. Day after day he had discovered what joys he had stupidly decided to sacrifice on the altar of work and how Robert's existence had given his life a new lease of life. All this Malcolm hadn't foreseen and had turned Vincent Konnor into the Achilles heel of the whole complex and pharaonic criminal project orchestrated in Soccer Town.

It had been a fatal mistake and now the man with a thousand faces was trying to hide everything, destroying Area 51.

The chip automatically disengaged from its housing. Daniel took it and put it safely in his pocket. He looked at that infernal machine with an air of defiance. Soon Malcolm's bombs would arrive there too and destroy it. 'One less job,' he thought. Because otherwise he would have done it.

He programmed his navigator and headed for the exit. A roar startled him: the bombs were early. A long, deep lesion had formed around the exit door, blocking it and leaving just six inches of opening. Impossible to get through.

Another explosion.

The violent shock wave threw him to the ground. Together with him, machinery, equipment, furniture, parts of walls and ceiling fell. Daniel tried to protect his head with his arms crossed, curling up.

An intense pain grabbed him in the right leg, forcing him to scream an excruciating scream. The mechanical arm of an analyser had fallen on him, blocking his limb.

The pain was strong. Probably he broke his leg, too. With the healthy one he pushed hard on the mechanical arm, in an attempt to free himself. He couldn't.

He fell to the ground on his side, towards the door. The last blast had knocked it down, opening a huge gap. A real hoax. Now that he could get out of that place, he was forced to wait for the inevitable fate on the floor.

A glint caught his attention. It came from a cylindrical container he hadn't noticed before. The outer cladding was probably metallic, because it reflected the light of the materials dangling from the gutted ceiling. It was a few feet away from him. It seemed unlabelled and it seemed very heavy.

In those moments of despair, an idea materialized, and it made sense to him. If he had been able to drop the container on the farthest section of the mechanical arm, perhaps the part blocking him would have stood up a bit, just enough to pull the leg out and release it.

He tried to get closer by putting pressure on one hand, then he tried to stretch forward as far as he could with a tug.

Nothing. He'd recovered a few centimetres, but it wasn't enough. He wanted to try again.

This time he would have prepared the gesture with some oscillations of the trunk, so as to favour the final effort. He began to bend the trunk back and forth, trying from time to time to increase the amplitude of the oscillation, getting closer and closer to his goal.

The time came.

Daniel gave the last kidney shot and charged up with a powerful scream.

This time he was able to push the steel container, but not as far as he wanted to. The shimmering object staggered forward and for a moment was undecided whether to fall or return to its initial position.

Daniel held his breath. They were endless moments.

Finally the centre of gravity of the container crossed the no return line and fell from the pedestal that housed it. The object hit as expected the far part of the mechanical arm, but with only one unexpected consequence: the impact had opened a small hole in the cylinder, now a gaseous and very dense, grey substance was coming out. By now on the ground, the metal container showed the label, the block letter 'HARMFUL' and the drawing of the skull with the crossed bones.

Otherwise, the mechanical arm hadn't moved an inch.

From the frying pan to the grill.

The gas had already saturated the area around the container, hiding it from the sight of its future victim. Daniel's eyes still looked around for anything that might suggest a solution.

He couldn't find any. The gap created by the exploding door did not help, as it overlooked a windowless corridor. There was no draught, so the gas wouldn't disperse.

That sort of dense grey mist had almost caught up with him. Daniel will breathe long and tighten his lips. He tried to relax. He knew he'd have to siphon the oxygen and get worked up would only burn a great deal of it unnecessarily.

The merciless reason told him it was over. He was alone, stuck. Any minute other explosions would have reduced the lab to a pile of rubble and buried it. If he was sure he wasn't in pain, he'd open his lips wide to end it right away. It was going to be his little revenge on fate. He would have decided, at least, the time to die and he would have passed on to a better life with dignity.

Survival instinct, on the other hand, ordered him to stay calm and continue to hold his breath. The will to live, just now that he had found friends and love, forced him not to lose hope.

It had already been over 70 seconds. The daily appointment with his Running Globe was giving him a few more moments of endurance, but Daniel knew it would only delay his agony.

Another explosion thundered inside the lab.

An entire wall collapsed on the Reset Machine, shattering it. Daniel was happy about it. And yet...

'It can't end like this,' he said. The memory chip, the only possible future for most of the forced tenants in Hidden City, risked being buried with him. The players who had not benefited from the optical shock were many, and they could not have found their identity without the chip that was inside his pocket.

Daniel was wondering whether or not Jerry belonged to that big group of footballers. Knowing he was already free of that sentence would have eased his burden of failure.

His thoughts were interrupted by another roar, this time much louder than before.

A large area of the ceiling fell on the other equipment. Even the incubator was dismembered into a thousand pieces. The metal part of an analyser splashed off after the deflagration.

Daniel suffered a stabbing pain in his right shoulder. That wreck had hit him. He tried to resist the pain and not to scream, gritting his teeth almost to the point of tearing a lip and further compressing the air as he tried to get out.

He barely squinted his lips to loosen the force that was attacking him from the inside. It was a terrible mistake. The lungs got the better of him and ejected the remaining oxygen-deprived contents.

Daniel tried to catch up a few seconds without inhaling. He stiffened his abdominal muscles to keep his diaphragm up. It would have helped him resist.

The view became blurred and the colours around him became confused. He was cracking up.

So the time had come. He let go of his sad fate and relaxed his jaw. His lips opened up, he could breathe again.

The gaseous mixture pervaded his lungs and, not containing oxygen, amplified the sense of suffocation already caused by forced apnoea.

He wasn't in pain. Suffering in his last moments of life had always been his greatest fear and, thank God, it was not materializing. He wanted to leave without noticing, and that's what was happening.

It was over.

Chapter 47

Most of the writings on life beyond life, read by Daniel in unsuspecting times, described that passage as a happy path. Almost all the testimonies of those who had returned described the passage in the same way: the soul separated from the body levitating on it and was then sucked into a tunnel that led to a strong light.

Daniel did not see any tunnel, nor his body from above, but he felt silence and a deep feeling of peace, of total relaxation.

After a few moments, that pleasant sense of abandonment began to dissolve under the blows of undefined sounds. One of them, among many, seemed to repeat itself over and over again and take on sharper and sharper contours. That was his name.

'Daniel!'

He had always thought that, after all, pre-mortem experiences were unreliable precisely because in the end they were not really passages. It was necessary to die in order to ascertain the truth and explore the great mystery, but this condition implied no return. Impossible, therefore, to rely on the words of the alleged witnesses.

'Professor Daniel!'

That voice again. That in the afterlife, he had never read the academic titles. Something wasn't right.

The awakening of leg pain accelerated the recovery of his sensory faculties. He could hear well now, but his vision was still blurry.

'Professor Daniel!'

He knew that voice.

'Professor Daniel!'

His eyes, just freed from a black rubber mask that someone had put on his face, now focused on the external environment. The voice that repeated his name gradually took on the increasingly clear-cut contours of a face that he remembered well.

'Detective Torst... Where am I?'

'You fainted, Professor. I saw you on my communicator and rushed over, managed to get you back with oxygen. When I arrived you were already unconscious.'

'The gas...' stammered Daniel with dry lips, still frightened.

'No more danger,' reassured Torst. 'The last explosion opened a door to the outside and the gas dispersed.'

Daniel coughed, pushed himself to his side and looked around. He was a few feet from the entrance to the lab where he got stuck. He tried to lift himself, but the pain prevented him.

'I think my leg is broken.'

'I think so, too. The thing you had on was pretty heavy. I was almost afraid I wouldn't be able to free you. The important thing now is to get away. Lean on me,' said the cop, helping him to get up while trying to hold on to the backpack he was still wearing. 'Professor, did you have time to retrieve the chip?' he asked while Daniel held a grimace of pain and wrapped his arm around his neck.

'Yes...it's in my jacket.'

'Perfect. Let's go. Your friends are waiting for us at Transport Sphere.'

With considerable difficulty the two began to gain metres. At the expense of the injured leg, Daniel tried not to put too much weight on the detective's gait, but it was still a burden for his escape partner.

They had walked barely ten metres and a thunderous explosion undermined their precarious balance.

Torst fell to the ground, dragging Daniel over him. The backpack acted as a buffer.

'Don't worry, Professor, I've come out of worse situations,' the detective reassured him by getting up. He shook off the dusty clothes and sketched a smile to ease the tension. 'We'll make it, Professor, we'll make it,' Torst said.

Daniel did not answer: his attention had been captured by an image that, until a few moments before, he never thought he would see again.

'Josie!' he exclaimed loudly, forgetting for a moment the pain in his leg.

Torst looked up and saw Thomas and Josie heading towards them.

'What are you doing here? I recommended that you wait for us at Transport Sphere,' the detective protested. In his heart, however, he thanked heaven for the unexpected help. Given the situation, and beyond the assurances given to the professor, he had strong doubts about the possibility of arriving in the east wing before Malcolm's bombs.

Now things were changing.

Josie stepped up and joined Daniel. She hugged him tight.

'What happened to your leg?' she asked thoughtfully, loosening her grip.

'It's broken, but it's not a problem now. We need to get out of this place. Now.'

Thomas approached his friend and smiled at him from the other side, lightening the weight on Torst's curved back. Josie, reluctantly, stepped aside and stood at the head of the column.

An explosion in the distance reminded the four fugitives of their precarious condition.

Torst gathered his strength and tried to pick up the pace. Thomas did the same.

'We are moments away from the transit area. It will be much easier to get to the Transport Sphere there,' the detective said to keep morale up. 'After the next intersection, there should be a tunnel through the suburbs.'

A rumble.

Josie accelerated her pace further to get to the next crossroads as quickly as possible.

A louder roar, a deflagration.

The explosion splashed some pieces of plaster, one of them hit Josie, who screamed and lost her balance. Thomas abandoned Daniel's grip. He left him momentarily attached to Torst's shoulder, and ran ten metres ahead to his friend's rescue.

'Are you all right, Josie?'

'It's all right, I've been smeared. It's nothing. It went well this time. Let's get the hell out of here.'

Josie got up right away. The thunder of yet another detonation ripped through the air. A portion of the floor suddenly collapsed, emitting flames from below that already lapped the ceiling. Thomas and Josie tried to rush back, but another piece of floor gave way and the two couples were separated by a fracture at least five metres long. On one side them, on the other Torst and Daniel. They looked at each other without saying anything, the situation was in front of everyone. Meanwhile, the smoke began to fill the hallway.

Detective Torst, used to dealing with emergencies for a living, was the first to respond.

'Professor, give me the chip,' he said resolutely.

Daniel obeyed. He took the chip out of his pocket and handed it to him.

Thomas and Josie stood by waiting to see what the cop's

plan was.

Torst placed Daniel on the ground, on his side, and opened the side pouch of his backpack. He pulled out a bigger laser pointer than the ones on the market. He placed the chip in a small lodging, which he closed with a click. Finally he fired in the direction of Josie and Thomas, recommending that they keep to one side.

A small black cylinder, just three centimetres long, stuck to the wall. Thomas retrieved it and put it safely in his jacket pocket.

'Mr Lewton, I'm giving you the chip with those guys' memories. You two have a better chance of getting out of this place than we do. All you have to do is go a few hundred metres.'

'We can't leave you here,' Thomas said, more with heart than reason.

'There must be a way through here!' Josie continued coughing.

'Go! The professor and I will be fine. I know another way, we just need to stretch the road a little bit.'

'Go! Quickly!' cried Daniel as he crossed Josie's eyes. His was a kind of plea. Josie understood.

'All right,' she stammered then, but she would much rather have stayed there.

Thomas grabbed her hand and dragged her away, after a few seconds they had already disappeared behind the first intersection. She turned for one last, silent look.

Left alone, Daniel asked Torst, 'There's no alternative passage, is there?'

'No. Not the way you imagine, at least,' confirmed Torst. 'Come with me, lean on.'

The two went back about fifty metres, into the Reset Machine room. Once there, the detective started fiddling with his backpack.

'Help me put this harness on you,' he ordered, observing the crack in the wall made by a previous explosion: the one that had dispersed the gas and, indirectly, saved the professor's life. Beyond, the blue sky and the dizzying abyss.

'What's your plan?'

'We're leaving, Professor, the only way out.'

Daniel still didn't understand.

Torst tightened the straps around his waist and then hooked his own. He took a few steps forward and took a look over the cliff.

Daniel understood.

'You won't want to...' he shyly asked.

'It's the only way, Professor.'

Torst approached Daniel. He helped him stand up and pulled his chest closer to his own. He crossed the straps by hooking them to each other and locking them with mechanic fasteners.

'How do you hope to make it, Detective?' Daniel asked again, this time with his heart in his throat and fear of knowing the answer.

'Thanks to an old parachute. Although it has been parked in history museums for over a hundred years, we special teams have always had it. They're the only ones that are magnetic interference-proof. That's how we're going to fool Malcolm and all his technology with a century old wreck.'

Torst gave the safeties the last check.

'Put the foot of your broken leg on mine and let me guide you, Professor.'

Daniel went along with it. He could feel his knees shaking and Torst noticed, but he ignored it.

A few movements and they were a stone's throw from the abyss.

'On the count of three, leverage your healthy leg and jump with me.'

'All right.'

'One!'

Daniel closed his eyes, filled his lungs and clenched his fists.

'Two!'

He reconsidered. He opened his eyes wide. He wanted to face his fate, whatever it was.

'Three!'

Torst and Daniel pushed forward.

Daniel felt the ground beneath his feet disappear. The body stretched out and was sucked down.

He instinctively issued a desperate cry of defiance to life, but this immediately flaked upwards.

There was only one thing around him now: emptiness.

Epilogue

Four years later

'Are you ready?'

'Of course. I've made arrangements to organize everything in the garden this year.'

'How come?'

'I did it for little Daniel. You can't keep an almost four-year-old child at home, listening to our usual speeches.'

'Great idea! That kid's a tornado. We can't suffocate him in here.'

'Did you get the answer from Manuel?'

'Yes. And he has some secret mission going on this time, too. He sent me the usual video message.'

Daniel approached Josie laterally, lifting the sleeve of his shirt a few inches to allow her to better see the display of his communicator. After a couple of finger movements, Manuel Torst's holographic face appeared.

'Hi, Professor! I'm sorry but I won't be able to be with you again this year. Labour commitments, the contents of which you can imagine, force me to give up Miss Carson's delicacies and your pretty lady-'s kind hospitality.'

Josie greeted Captain Torst's compliments with a smile.

'Please give my regards to Jerry, Thomas, Robert and Katrine. I'll try my best to be with you next year. I'll see you soon.'

The holographic pixels were slabbed until the image dissolved. Daniel lowered his arm.

'I would have liked to have him here, but we can forgive him. He deserves it, don't you think? We owe him a lot,' commented Daniel.

'I'll be grateful to him all my life. He gave me my pain in the ass in one piece,' she continued, approaching her chest to her husband's and touching his face with her forehead.

Josie still had in her mind, as clear as four years earlier, the image of Daniel emerging from the clouds of smoke at Area 51 in the company of Detective Torst.

The two had managed to get away with that obsolete parachute and, despite the ruinous landing, they had managed to land safely. The special ops team had done the rest.

Daniel accepted his wife's obvious invitation and responded with a kiss.

Josie felt like she was reliving the same kiss that they had exchanged in the rubble of Area 51 on that famous 5th February, as soon as she was allowed to hug him again.

A little cough, a few feet behind them, interrupted the flashback. Through the studio door was Miss Carson who, embarrassed at the inopportune moment when she entered, was waiting for the right moment to intrude.

Daniel pulled his lips apart and turned to her and said.

'Miss Carson, do you need anything? Tell me.'

'Mr and Mrs Konnor called. They'll be here by thirteen.'

'What about Jerry and Thomas?'

'They've confirmed they'll arrive at the appointed time.'

'Good. Since we're in the garden, have you had some toys set up for little Daniel?'

'Sure. I also had a special menu prepared for the child.'

'Always impeccable. Thank you!'

'We'll be there soon,' Josie added, dismissing the housekeeper.

What followed the destruction, not just material destruction, of Area 51 had been hot and hectic days throughout the state. The Soccer Town scandal had held up for weeks, in the media, creating serious political problems for the government at the time, accused by the opposition of failing to keep a serious watch and of allowing criminals to put on that disgraceful farce.

The efforts to avoid the fall of the government had found in Robert Konnor a valid protagonist, strong in his popularity and charisma. To gain credibility, the President had placed Robert in charge of the reconstruction first, and the management afterwards, of the new Soccer Town.

Daniel Keaton's life, too, after those four hellish days, had been turned upside down. Definitely for the better. He had found the woman he'd always loved, with whom he was wedded. He had recovered his friend Jerry. He had acquired a brother and also a nephew: Robert and Katrine, by mutual agreement, had wanted to give his name to their child, to seal the bond that had united them in an indissoluble, albeit daring way.

The 5th February was a special date for all of them, as well as a regular appointment at Villa Keaton. There were several events to celebrate or remember: the escape from Area 51, the reorganization of the quartet with the return of Jerry, the liberation of all the guys in Hidden City, back to life after regaining their memories. But in general, the only real reason was the desire to be together.

The 5th February of that year had a special flavour compared to previous ones because Daniel and Josie would tell friends that they were waiting for the heir to the Keaton house.

The news had already filled their hearts for a few weeks but, after initial hesitations about whether or not to know the sex of the unborn child, only that morning Josie had decided for yes.

Daniel would have preferred a male, at the same time he hoped it would be a female to prevent her from one day taking too much interest in the world of football. He didn't want to find himself, with roles reversed, in the position that thirty-three years earlier had been his father's. More than a rational assessment, it was a kind of unconscious fear.

'Where were we?' Daniel regained his lips.

'I've taken the test!' Josie suddenly fired, cooling her husband's boils.

The future daddy tried to keep the sense of turmoil that had caught him from leaking out, but he didn't succeed. In those cases he was an open book.

'So?' he replied, waiting for the important news.

Josie enjoyed a few more seconds of waiting. She enjoyed keeping him on his toes.

Daniel was dying to know and yet he flaunted an almost unselfish air. It was a little game he often played when he didn't want to give her the satisfaction.

Josie understood at once, yet she preferred not to delay. This time it wasn't the usual spitefulness, or a fringe event, but a basic piece of their family's future.

She gave the answer.

'It's a girl.'

'Did you check out our precious treasure, Jennifer?'
'Of course, Simon. The embryos are in excellent health.'
'I had no doubt about your efficiency.'
'Neither do I.'

Author's note

I also thank:

my children Simona and Vincenzo for the unconditional affection they show me; my father Enzo and my mother Antonietta who, from down here and from up there, support me in silence; lastly, my editor Wolf Graham for his trust in me.

Lightning Source UK Ltd.
Milton Keynes UK
UKHW012324150920
369943UK00001B/157